THE
RIVER
GHOST

BOOKS BY DAWN MERRIMAN

RYLAN FLYNN MYSTERY SERIES

The Spirit Girls

The Shadow Girls

The Whisper House

The Haunted Child

THE
RIVER
GHOST

DAWN MERRIMAN

SECOND SKY

Published by Second Sky in 2024

An imprint of Storyfire Ltd.
Carmelite House
50 Victoria Embankment
London EC4Y 0DZ
United Kingdom

www.secondskybooks.com

Storyfire Ltd's authorised representative in the EEA is Hachette Ireland
8 Castlecourt Centre
Castleknock Road
Castleknock
Dublin 15 D15 YF6A
Ireland

ISBN: 978-1-83618-273-3
eBook ISBN: 978-1-83618-272-6

This book is dedicated to my husband, Kevin.
Thank you for all your help and your constant support.
I could not write these stories without you.

ONE

RYLAN FLYNN

The light on the bridge burns my eyes. I lift my hand to block the light and pull closer to the side of the bridge to let the car pass. The light doesn't move, just glows brighter until it fills the bridge.

The tingle in my back tells me it's not a car. It's a spirit.

The light focuses and I see a woman.

The glowing woman points over the metal side to the dark water below.

"There's a ghost here." I tell Mickey in the passenger seat. "She's trying to show me something."

I climb out of the car, into the quiet of late night, the only sound from the moving water below. The woman still points, her loose hair hanging down her back over her white dress. When she turns, I see something hanging from her neck.

It's a rope, tied tight against her throat.

I look from the rope to her worried eyes.

"Show me," I tell her.

She seems surprised I can see her, but recovers quickly, leading us across the bridge. We climb around the guard rail toward the river's edge.

Mickey follows with the camera we use to film our YouTube show. We slip and slide down the bank.

At one point, Mickey loses her footing and almost drops the camera. I grab her arm, steadying her.

"Careful," I whisper, remembering she can't benefit from the light of the spirit leading us. She regains her footing and walks to the narrow river's edge.

"What are we doing down here? Do you see anything?" She turns on the camera light and shines it up and down the bank.

The woman's ghost points again, this time to a pile of branches under the bridge. Mickey pans the light in the direction I tell her.

Among the branches, a bare foot sticks out from the water.

The camera light wavers as Mickey gasps. "Is that..."

"It's okay," I say, as much to myself as to Mickey. I rub Mickey's shoulder, then turn to the ghost for answers.

The riverbank is dark—the ghost is gone.

I pull out my phone light and approach the foot, its pink painted toes pointing to the sky.

She lays face up underwater, her dark hair tangled in the branches. She's dressed in a long-sleeve tee and black leggings. Both her feet are bare, one sticking out of the water, the other hidden beneath a heavy branch.

My stomach lurches at the sight. I step back, unsteady as my feet sink into the soft edges of the river. My heart hammers.

"It's a young woman," I tell Mickey. "We need to call this in." I try for control over the situation, and my reaction.

I glance back at the woman under the water, shine my light on her face. A tiny crab crawls across her open lips, then disappears into her mouth.

I have to look away as my mouth waters and I nearly vomit.

"We need Ford and Tyler," Mickey says, breathless. "They'll know what to do."

I reach in my pocket for my phone, only to realize it's

already in my hand. I can't get my fingers to work, they're shaking too badly.

"Siri, call Ford."

He answers on the first ring.

"Hello, beautiful," he says sleepily. I must have woken him.

"Hey," I start. "We, um, we were filming, and we found a ghost on the old trestle bridge on Ostermeyer Road."

"That's good, isn't it?" I hear blankets rustling and picture him sitting up in bed.

"We found—" I don't want to say these words. Don't want the poor girl under the river to be real. Once I start, the words pour out. "We found the body of a woman under the bridge. Her foot was sticking out. When I looked, she was tangled in some branches. There was a crab. "My voice breaks. I suck in a deep breath.

"Stay put. I'll call it in. Rylan, just hang tight and I'll be right there." The care in his voice calms my ragged emotions.

"We'll be here. Ford, thank you."

"Just wait for me and don't touch anything," he says gently. "I'll be quick."

I hang up and feel Mickey watching me. When I turn, her eyes are wide.

"They're coming," I tell her.

"Something's different with you two," she says.

She's right, Ford and I *are* different. We finally realized our feelings. Well, he realized. I've been half in love with him most of my life. It's all so new, I haven't even told Mickey yet. "Maybe." I shrug one shoulder.

I glance at the pile of branches again. This is not the time or place to get into my love life. Mickey realizes that too and we wait in silence, listening to the rustle of the narrow river and the wind in the trees that line the top of each bank. The frogs sing their eternal song. Under different circumstances, it would be a lovely night.

"How long do you think she's been down here?" Mickey asks after a while.

"She's in pretty good condition, so probably not too long. The coroner will be able to tell."

"Too bad he has to come. He won't be happy to see you again."

That's an understatement. Dr. Marrero is not my biggest fan.

"It's not my fault the ghost on the bridge stopped us," I point out.

"Is she still here? Maybe she can tell us what happened."

When I think about it, I can feel a twinge in my back. I look up to the bridge and see her light shining. "She's up there. Let's go find out."

Mickey follows me, slipping up the bank to the bridge, where the woman is pacing. Mickey turns the camera on, and I go to work.

"Hello," I say gently. "Can we talk?"

The woman stops her pacing and stares at me in wonder. "You can see me?"

"Yes."

"And hear me?"

"It's a gift," I say with a slight smile. "What's your name?"

"Hazel." She runs her hands down her pale dress, which looks like something from the 1940s. Her fingers glide over the rope as if to hide it. "What's that?" She points to Mickey's camera.

"This is my friend, Mickey, and that's her video camera. We make a kind of television show about ghosts. Do you mind if we film this?"

"I don't mind, but I've never seen anything like that. Like the movies."

Hazel steps close to Mickey, studying the camera. "She's interested in your camera," I tell Mickey.

"Why do you make a show?" Hazel asks. "Do people really watch it?"

I repeat the questions for the camera. To my surprise, Mickey answers. "We make the show to help people. Well, ghosts actually. See, Rylan has helped many spirits cross over to the other side. We recently got very popular with a mother and son we helped cross."

Hazel circles Mickey, reaches toward her curly hair. "This one can't hear me, can she?" Hazel asks.

"She's very close to you, Mickey. Don't move. Mickey can't hear or see you, but she believes," I tell Hazel. "She helps me all the time."

Hazel comes around to the front of the camera, looks directly into the lens. "This thing can't see me either?"

"Only I can see you. I have another friend named Jamie that could probably hear you, but that's it."

"Interesting." Hazel turns her attention back to me. "Pleased to meet you both. And your camera. It has been very lonely here. Nobody passing by has ever seen or talked to me before. I try to talk to the young people that come to the river, but no one answers."

Hazel looks over the bridge to the water below.

I tell Mickey and the camera what she said. "I've heard this is a hangout for teenagers. They like to jump off the bridge into the water, right?"

"Teenagers, kids with their parents. They all come in the summer. No one has been here lately. Too cold."

"Did the young woman down there come to jump too?"

A shadow passes over Hazel's eyes. "She didn't jump. I don't know where she came from. I'm not here all the time. Sometimes, I'm—well, I'm not here. When I got back, she was down there." She points over the side of the bridge. "I tried to stop any car that came by. It's so late at night, I'd about given up when you came. I really didn't think you'd stop."

"So you found her tonight?"

"No, last night. I've kept watch over her, not that anyone can protect her now."

"Is she here? Her spirit, I mean." I look up and down the river, hoping for a glimmer of the young woman in the river.

"I haven't seen anything like that, not here."

"Hazel, why are you here?" I ask gently. "Did something happen to you on this bridge?" I motion toward the rope.

She reaches for the rope, touches it nervously.

"I, um. I kind of died here."

"On this bridge? What happened?"

"I was to be married. This is my wedding dress." She smooths the white fabric. "I waited at the church, but Bart didn't come. My whole family was there, our friends. It was humiliating. I didn't know what to do without him." She wipes at her eyes. "I came here with this rope I took from Daddy's barn. It was stupid. I knew that as soon as I jumped, but it was too late then."

"And you've been here ever since?"

"All alone. Much more alone than I would have been without Bart. I'd give anything to take it back." Her voice breaks. "But I can't. My mother used to come here to visit, in the beginning. That was sort of nice, even if she couldn't hear or see me. She'd cry a lot, which hurt to watch. Daddy even came once, but I don't think Mom knew. He got mad and yelled, although he didn't know I was here either. After a long while, they stopped coming. At first, I thought they forgot me, then I realized they'd probably died too. I hoped they'd come as spirits, but they never did."

Hazel stops talking when a car approaches.

I recognize the black Malibu. Ford has arrived.

TWO

RYLAN FLYNN

"You think she was murdered?" Hazel asks sadly. "I was afraid of that."

Ford parks his car behind my old tan Cadillac, then walks our way. Despite the situation, a surge of excitement courses through my veins. I wonder if he feels it too.

Then the questions start in my head.

How do we act now?

What do I say?

"Hey," I say lamely when he gets close.

"Hey," he replies, a bit awkward, his hands in his pockets.

"Now there's a cute one," Hazel says, admiring Ford. "You say he's the police?" She walks around him, looking closely. "We didn't have police like this in my day."

"Leave him alone," I say, a little too sharply.

Hazel looks up, startled. "I get it. This one's yours. I'll leave you to it." She moves away down the bridge.

Ford notices the camera. "Filming?" he asks.

"We were talking to the ghost that led us to the body. Her name is Hazel. She's over there."

He looks over his shoulder to the far end of the bridge. "Did she see what happened?"

"No. She said the body just showed up while she was gone last night. She's been trying to flag someone down ever since, but I was the first one to see her."

"Right. Of course."

He seems nervous. I wonder how we're supposed to greet each other now. My lips yearn for his, but this is not the time or place.

Mickey puts the camera down, then eyes me suspiciously. I feel my cheeks burn under her scrutiny.

An awkward pause hangs in the air, above the sound of singing frogs.

"Where is she?" Ford finally breaks the tension.

"She's down here," I say, pointing over the side of the bridge. We all look over the side. In the pale moonlight, the only thing visible of the woman is her pink painted toenails.

After a long moment, Ford says, "Let's stay up here until the rest of them come. I don't want to contaminate the scene."

"We went down," Mickey says. "Sorry about that."

"We didn't know," I add.

"That's okay," he says, as red and blue lights appear down Ostermeyer Road. A personal car follows the cruiser, driving fast. "That should be Tyler," Ford says.

The cruiser's lights fill the darkness of the bridge. Ford's partner, Detective Tyler Spencer, parks behind it. The officer waits for Tyler to reach him, then joins our little group.

"Hey, Rylan. I guess I should be surprised," Officer James Frazier says. "Hey, Mickey. She getting you into trouble again?" Frazier's hostility is barely in check. We have a rocky relationship. He tends to show up when I don't want him to, and he'd prefer I stayed home and out of the way.

"Jimmy," I say, using the nickname he went by in middle school. "Working the night shift again?"

I didn't mean it as a dig, but he bristles a bit. "You two running around in the middle of the night again?" he asks.

For a moment, I fear he's talking about Ford and me "running around," then realize he means Mickey.

"We were trying to cross over a ghost back at the storage units," Mickey says. "He refused to go."

Down the bridge, I hear Hazel make a sound of surprise. I look at her curiously, but she turns her back.

"We were driving home when a ghost flagged us down," Mickey continues.

"A ghost?" Frazier asks. "You still doing that little show of yours?"

"It's not little anymore," Mickey says. "Our last episode is getting tons of views. Looks like we're going viral." She lifts her chin and stares him down.

"That's nice," Frazier says dismissively.

"If you're done harassing the witnesses," Tyler says, "can we get to the reason we're all here?" He gives Frazier a hard look.

"The body is down in the river," Ford explains. "Frazier, you wait up here, and don't let anyone down without our permission." Ford heads for the end of the bridge. Frazier looks over the side, then straightens his belt, obviously not pleased to be left out.

"Rylan, you and Mickey stay here, too," Tyler adds, then he follows Ford off the bridge to the steep bank.

Mickey joins me in watching over the side, as does Hazel.

"What's going to happen now?" Hazel asks, all abuzz. "There's never any excitement like this around here."

"They will examine the body. Then the crime-scene techs will come and scour the area for any evidence of what happened to her. At some point, the coroner will come to look things over and take the body to his lab."

"Interesting," Hazel says.

"Hazel is very curious," I tell Mickey.

"So am I," she says. "This is all so sad, though. That poor woman is family to someone. Wonder if they've missed her. Maybe there's a missing person's report on her."

"Maybe," I say.

We watch as Ford and Tyler slide down the bank to the river's edge. They both have flashlights—the beams shine on the foot sticking out of the river.

Ford creeps closer, his light shining on the face under the water. I hope the crab has gone. The memory of it being in her mouth makes me shiver.

Ford leans closer to the body, then stands up with a shout. "No!" he cries into the night.

Tyler shines his light on her, then looks at Ford in confusion. "What's wrong?"

I lean over the side, drawn to the man I love and the pain in that one word.

"It's Kenzie," Ford says so quietly I can barely hear him.

"Kenzie? You know her?"

"Mackenzie Odell. She's my cousin." Ford turns away from the body, searching for my face high above him. I meet his eyes —the suffering I see in the moonlight slices at my heart.

"No," I whisper, searching my memories for a Kenzie. I come up with nothing.

"She's my aunt's stepdaughter," Ford says to me. He wipes at his face, steps away from the river's edge.

I'm so focused on Ford I don't realize Dr. Marrero is suddenly by my side. "Flynn. Another body?" he asks.

I tear my eyes from Ford. "It's Ford's cousin," I say breathlessly.

Marrero looks down to Ford and Tyler. "You know the victim?" Marrero asks. "She's your family?"

"My mom's sister's stepdaughter. Yes, family."

"Then get out of there. You can't be on this case if she's family." Marrero's tone brooks no argument.

"I won't step away," Ford argues anyway.

"You must and you will. Do I need to bring Chief McKay in on this?"

Ford hangs his head, then turns to Tyler, helpless. "Don't worry. I've got it," Tyler says, patting Ford on the back.

"But I—"

"I know," Tyler says. "I'm so sorry for your loss."

Crime scene techs are now descending the bank, following Marrero. "Out of my crime scene," the coroner says.

Ford can only obey. As the techs get to work, Ford climbs the bank back to the bridge. I go to him.

"I'm so sorry," I say. "Did you know her well?"

"Not really. My Aunt Tammy married her dad a few years back. I saw Kenzie at Christmas and stuff like that. She's young. So young. Maybe twenty." He rubs his face in distress. "This is going to kill her father. Owen is a good man. I was so happy for Aunt Tammy when she finally found him. She took Kenzie in as her own. They were a happy family." He makes a sound of pain that shakes me.

Not caring who is watching, I wrap him in my arms and hold him close. "I'm sorry, Ford."

"We need to get to them, to Tammy and Owen. I want them to hear this from me."

"I understand. You're sure it's her? I mean, she's under water. And it's dark."

He leans his forehead against mine. "It's her." He sounds broken.

"You going to kiss him or what?" Hazel asks. I'm glad no one can hear her, but I realize that Mickey, Frazier and the tech Tyler is friendly with, Michelle, are all watching us. Mickey and Michelle have sympathetic looks on their faces. Frazier's face seems angry.

"I'm sorry," Frazier says, though he doesn't sound sorry.

"This is an active crime scene. You three will have to leave." He nods to Mickey, Ford and me.

Ford glares at him, but heads to his car. He turns to me. "Will you come? I could use your help."

Mickey puts a hand on the back of my shoulder. "I can take the Caddy. You go with Ford."

She gives me a knowing look.

"Thank you," I say genuinely, then follow Ford through the dark to his Malibu.

It's the first time I've been in his car. It smells like coffee mixed with his cologne—a pleasant scent.

"I'm so sorry about your cousin," I say as I settle into the car. "I don't know what to say."

Ford puts the car in drive, then guns the gas. "Tell me you'll help me investigate."

"Investigate? You heard Marrero. You're not working this case."

He turns his head and meets my gaze. "That never stopped you before. We're going to find the person who did this."

THREE

RYLAN FLYNN

The dark fields stretch around us, broken by tree lines and fence rows. I focus on the fields, on the stars, on the farms. Anything to not think of the young woman under the bridge.

Eventually, I turn to Ford. His hand rests on the gear shifter and I place mine on top.

"I don't know what to say," I repeat, trying to fill the deafening silence.

"I know. I don't either."

"Tell me about Kenzie."

Even in the dark, I can see him smile. "Like I said, I didn't know her well, but she always made me laugh. Last Christmas we were all at Grandma Delia's, and Kenzie sat down at the piano and started playing Christmas songs, singing really loud. It didn't take long until we joined her. It was a corny thing, but it was a good memory."

"She sounds wonderful."

"She had a good heart. I heard she'd gotten into some trouble a while back, so she moved here from Fort Wayne to live with her dad. She did okay then, had even been going to the community college. But she dropped out. I remember Mom talking about it. Aunt Tammy was worried for her. Said she was acting differently."

I think about this for a few moments. "Could it have been drugs?" I ask gently.

Ford looks at me seriously. "I hate to think that, but yeah. It could have been. It happens all the time.

"So she lives here with her dad and your aunt? Where's her mom?"

"Still in Fort Wayne." Ford grows quiet as the lights of Ashby grow in the sky ahead, and the houses get closer together. He turns down a narrow road that leads to a small neighborhood, then pulls up in front of a modest two-story on a cul-de-sac. The only light on is a single bulb over the front door.

"If she lives with them, why didn't they report her missing?" I ask quietly. "You haven't had any reports, have you?"

"No," he says thoughtfully, looking at the dark house.

"Hazel said she found her last night. That's at least twenty-four hours she's been gone."

"A ghost is probably not the best judge of time," Ford points out.

"True. It's just curious."

"Aunt Tammy and Uncle Owen would never have hurt Kenzie," Ford says, his tone turned hard.

"I'm not saying that," I protest. "I'm just wondering why they didn't report her."

Ford grabs the door handle. "Let's just stick to what we know. Kenzie is dead. That's enough news for one night."

"I'm sorry, Ford. My mind's just reeling."

Ford doesn't open the door. Instead, he turns to me. "I know. I'm sorry too. We need to be together in this." He reaches for my cheek, runs his palm along my skin. "I'm glad you're here with me."

"I am too. This has to be so hard."

"It's never easy, but this is the first time I've had to give a death notice to family."

He turns back to the house, steels himself, then throws open the door.

The little neighborhood only has about ten houses in it. Beyond the back yards are more fields. The night is quiet, the only sound a dog barking far in the distance.

"Kind of creepy," I whisper. I do a mental check of my body to see if there's a tingle from a spirit. Luckily, I don't feel anything. I need all my attention focused on Ford and what we're here to do.

We make our way to the porch, side-by-side on the narrow walk. When we reach the front door, Ford raises his hand to press the bell—then hesitates.

"I don't want to do this," he says, dropping his hand. "Once I press this button, their whole life will never be the same. Tammy and Owen don't deserve this. Kenzie doesn't deserve this."

"We can still leave. Let Tyler do the notice."

Ford takes a deep breath. "No. I owe it to Aunt Tammy and my whole family that the news comes from me, not a stranger." Before he can change his mind, he stabs at the doorbell.

We can hear the chime inside, but the house is still. We wait for an answer, then he presses the bell again.

A light flips on in an upstairs window.

My stomach sinks. I've never done this—I wish I hadn't agreed to come.

Ford looks at me and his face is pale.

I need to do this for him.

"It will be okay," I whisper, though I know it won't.

Another light turns on, this time on the first floor, just inside the entry.

The lock unbolts with a scratch of metal and the door opens a few inches. A man's face peers out. "What in the world? It's the middle of the night," Uncle Owen grumbles. He throws the door open when he sees Ford. "Ford, what are you doing here?"

Behind Owen a woman—I assume to be Aunt Tammy—looks around his shoulder. She steps back when she sees Ford, then glances at me. "What's going on?" she breathes, grasping the neckline of her robe.

"Can we come in?" Ford croaks out.

Tammy and Owen look from Ford to me, panic taking over. Tammy locks eyes on mine. I have to look away.

Owen leads us into the living room, he and his wife sit on a gray couch full of pillows. Ford sits on a chair and I stand behind him, my shaking hands resting on the back.

"Please tell me this isn't about Kenzie," Owen says. "I called her yesterday and she never answered." His face grows red. "Please."

"I'm so sorry," Ford starts. "We found Kenzie's body tonight."

Tammy screams and covers her face. Owen begins shaking and leans back on the couch.

"What are you saying?" Tammy shrieks. "You have to be wrong. Kenzie isn't dead."

"What happened?" Owen asks. "A car accident?"

Tears sting my eyes as Ford says, "Not an accident." He stops and swallows hard. "We think she was murdered."

Tammy cries out again and Owen jumps from his seat. "That's not possible. No one would hurt Kenzie. You're wrong. It isn't her."

"I saw her myself," Ford says quietly. "I'm so sorry. I wanted you to hear it from me, so we came right here. They're working the scene now."

"Where?" Owen paces the room. "Where is my baby girl?"

"You can't go to the scene," Ford warns. "They won't let you see her. It might ruin evidence."

"Evidence? My daughter is not evidence!" Owen bellows in

pain. "She's lovely and bright and full of love." He suddenly stops pacing and his knees buckle. Ford jumps to help him back to the couch.

The room is filled with the sound of crying, no one knowing what to say now. "I'm so sorry for your loss," I say awkwardly.

"Who are you?" Tammy demands, pulling a gray throw pillow to her chest. "Why are you here?"

I don't know how to answer, and look to Ford.

"She's my—she's with me. Rylan helps us with cases sometimes."

"You're going to find out who killed my girl?" Owen asks, his voice pleading.

"I'm going to do all I can," I say.

"You'll catch this monster, right?" Tammy asks Ford.

"I will do everything in my power. I'm not technically on the case, since Kenzie is family."

"We need you," Tammy croaks. "I don't trust anyone else."

"Rylan and I will do what we can. I won't let whoever did this get away. I promise."

I'm surprised to hear Ford promise. Detectives never promise justice. It's not in their power to solve them all.

He feels me staring at him but waves me off. "This is different. I owe it to them."

Tammy and Owen are holding each other's hands and leaning against each other. Their grief fills the room. It's horrible to watch.

I feel a sudden rush of grief over losing my own mother to murder. After two years, it hasn't gotten any easier. Even with her ghost living in my house to keep me company, knowing she is dead to everyone else breaks my heart.

"We need to call Julia, her mother," Owen says. "She needs to know."

"Do you want me to call her?" Ford offers.

Owen straightens his back. "No. I need to do it. Just tell me —did she suffer? Was it a fast death?"

"We don't know for sure yet. I didn't see any outward signs of trauma."

"Did he..." Tammy can't finish the question.

"She was fully clothed," Ford says. "No obvious signs of sexual assault."

Tammy and Owen both breathe sighs of relief. "How did he... Was she shot?"

"I don't know yet. I really don't have much information at this point." He slips into his professional voice. "I'm sure Detective Tyler Spencer will be by this morning; he'll have more information and can answer your questions. I'm sorry, I was shooed off the scene once I made the identification."

Owen puts his arm around Tammy as she cries quietly. There doesn't seem to be anything else to say right now.

"We should go," I say.

"I'll be in touch tomorrow," Ford tells them. "I have lots of questions, but this isn't the time."

"Thank you," Owen says, not looking up.

Ford and I let ourselves out into the night. Once we're alone, I let the emotions out and my chest hurts. "That was awful," I whisper, "Is it always like that?"

"Usually I don't know those involved, but yes, it's always a terrible thing."

I reach for his hand and press it to my hot cheek. "I'm so sorry, Ford. I can't say that enough."

"Just help me find out the truth. They deserve to know what happened to their daughter."

"What do we do now?"

He looks at the moon and then toward the east. The sky is just beginning to turn pink. I'm suddenly exhausted, but I don't want to stop.

"We need to talk to her mom, Julia." He sighs heavily. "Want to take a drive into Fort Wayne?"

FOUR

RYLAN FLYNN

We drive through Ashby as the sun starts to glint in the sky. The streets are mostly empty at this hour, only a few cars and a woman out jogging, her ponytail swaying. We don't talk much, both of us lost in different forms of grief.

I can't stop thinking of my mother. The usual questions of who shot her reel through my mind. And I get nowhere with that line of thought.

Then Kenzie's face and the crab in her mouth flashes in my memory—I flinch.

"You okay?" Ford asks, seeing my sudden movement.

"Yeah. I mean no. I mean, I guess so. It's just so awful. I hate to think what your family will have to go through with her loss. It was bad enough losing my mom, but Kenzie had her whole life ahead of her."

Ford reaches for my hand and gives it a squeeze. "I appreciate you being here, helping me. My whole family will appreciate it."

"It's strange. I've known you most of my life, but I haven't met any of your family, except your mom."

"These aren't the greatest circumstances, that's for sure."

"You think Owen called Julia and told her the news already?" I ask.

"Most likely."

"Do you think she'll talk to us? She doesn't know us, and you're not actually on the case now."

"That's a good point." Ford glances out the side window, then turns the wheel, taking a turn that doesn't lead to the highway and Fort Wayne.

"Where are we going?"

"Grandma Delia's. She'll be up this early and I need to tell her. To be honest, I'd just like to see her. She and Kenzie were pretty close, ever since Kenzie came to town." Ford smiles slightly. "You'll love Grandma Delia. She's a character."

"I'm sure I will." I know Delia from reputation only. She's a realtor, has been for as long as I can remember. Her picture is on a bench across from Aunt Val's shop. The picture hasn't changed in years. Her hair is up in a fashionable bun, and she wears pearls in the photo. I've often wondered about her, being Ford's grandma, but I haven't met her officially. She came into The Hole once when I was helping Aunt Val a few years ago. She looked so glamorous in a smart pant suit. I was a bit tongue-tied at the time. I hope she doesn't remember me.

Grandma Delia lives in one of the first houses built in Ashby. The brick walls of the two-story are covered with ivy. A wide porch is flanked by brick columns with small lions on top. A light is on inside.

"Looks like she's up," Ford says. "I figured she would be. Aunt Tammy must have already called her."

Ford looks to the house with affection.

"You just want to see her, don't you?" I ask.

"Is that strange? We're very close. And I kind of want to get her take on this. Maybe she knows something that will help the investigation."

I'm a little jealous. "I wish I was that close to my grandparents. Mom's parents are gone, and my other grandparents live in South Carolina. I've never been that close to any of them."

The front door on the brick house opens and Delia walks out. "Ford, I knew you'd stop by. Are you coming in or not?" she calls.

A small smile creeps across his face. "Nothing gets past her."

I follow Ford up the walk toward Delia. She looks totally different than her bench. Her hair is loose and long, much grayer than the bun in the photo. Instead of pearls and a pant suit, she wears a deep red bath robe. If she's surprised to see Ford with a woman, she hides her reaction.

"Grandma Delia, this is Rylan Flynn."

"I know who she is. I watch your show, Rylan." She reaches a hand to shake. Her grip is stronger than I expect from such long, thin fingers. "Welcome. Wish we were meeting under better circumstances." Her voice is raspy and her eyes are pink. She must have been crying.

"Did Tammy call you?" Ford asks.

Delia takes Ford into her arms. "Yes. Good Lord, what an awful thing."

Ford is only an inch or so taller than Delia and his head rests on her shoulder. This is a side of him I've never seen. I like it.

When he finally lets go, she says, "Come in. Come in. I only have a few minutes, though. I told Tammy I'd come over. I think your mom is going too."

"That's good," Ford says.

Delia reaches for my hand again and leads me up the steps. "Welcome, Rylan. So how long have you two been dating?"

The question makes me freeze on the steps. "I—"

"Oh honey, Ford can't fool me." She looks over her shoulder at him. "That boy is smitten. Plus, you're with him at a time like this. You must be very important to him."

"I'm helping with the investigation," I try. "I found Kenzie last night."

"Oh, dear. What a horrible thing to experience. I'm glad you found her, though. Where was that again?"

"We haven't released that information," Ford says as we enter the house's wide foyer. Woodwork surrounds us in a welcoming embrace. The house smells like coffee and vanilla.

"Released the information," Delia repeats sarcastically. "This isn't an official visit, you can tell me."

"I didn't tell Owen and Aunt Tammy."

"I won't say anything to them." Delia leads us into a kitchen full of more woodwork. Even the counters are wood. She waves toward the breakfast nook, and I sit down.

"I'll let you have coffee, but only if you give me all the details," she says, getting cups out of a cabinet.

Ford sinks into the chair next to mine. "This is between us," he starts, then explains how Kenzie was found.

Delia fills coffee cups as she listens, hands them to us, then sits too. She looks at me. "A ghost led you to her? How interesting." She sips her coffee.

"It's what she does," Ford says, a bit defensive.

Delia's eyes widen. "I know that. I just find it fascinating how all this works. I never miss an episode of the show. The whole supernatural world is amazing."

"Mom told me that Kenzie was maybe in a little trouble. She dropped out of college?"

"That's what I heard, but I don't know the specifics. I do know she recently moved out of Tammy's and into an apartment of her own. A small run-down studio, the way Tammy explained it. She didn't understand why Kenzie would choose to move out of their house and into that."

"Do you know where the apartment is?" Ford asks.

"It's in the attic of a house over on Spring. One of those old houses that have been changed into multi-family units."

"Spring Street is definitely not the best neighborhood. I can see why Tammy wasn't happy about it."

"Tammy said it wasn't the only thing different. Kenzie has started being secretive. Not answering calls, that kind of thing."

"Interesting," Ford says. "Was she dating anyone?"

"Now I wouldn't know that. I loved Kenzie, but we weren't that kind of close. A pretty girl like her, I'm sure she had a boyfriend or two."

Delia's eyes flick to me, then back to her coffee. She drinks the rest of the cup, then stands. "Now, I must get dressed and go. Tammy needs me."

Ford and I stand too. "Of course," Ford says. "Thank you for sitting with us a little. It means a lot to me."

Delia kisses Ford on the cheek. "Anything for you, dear." She focuses on me. "You take care of him, now. He's a keeper."

"I will," I say. It feels strange talking out loud about having feelings for Ford.

"If you think of anything else, please call me," Ford says. "Rylan and I will be working this case, whether I'm supposed to or not."

Delia opens the front door for us. "You know, there was one strange thing. Kenzie always wore a lot of makeup, you know. Kind of dark with lots of eyeliner."

"I remember," Ford says.

"The last time I saw her, she didn't have any makeup on. We went to dinner with Tammy and Owen. You'd think she would have put on makeup."

Ford doesn't seem to know what to do with this information. "Okay."

"It's probably nothing. But it was a change."

"Thank you for the coffee." Ford kisses her cheek.

Delia suddenly pulls me into a hug. "Nice to meet you officially," she says near my ear, then lets me go.

When we're out on the walk, Ford says, "I think she likes you."

"I hope so."

He checks his watch. "Still want to go to Fort Wayne? I'm sure Owen has had time to call Kenzie's mom by now."

"Good. I don't think I can go through another notice like that," I say seriously.

"I know. It doesn't get easier."

"You have a hard job," I say as we climb into the car.

"It definitely is a challenge, but I wouldn't change it for anything. The way I look at it, I get to help people when they are at their very worst time. When I can close a case and bring justice, it makes it all worth it."

"I know what you mean," I say honestly. "The little bit of experience I've had has been very meaningful."

Ford stares at me in wonder. "I almost feel sorry for whoever hurt Kenzie."

"Why's that?"

"Because together, we are going to find him. And then God help him."

FIVE

TYLER SPENCER

I watch Rylan and Ford get in his car and drive away off the bridge. My heart goes out to him. Our job is hard enough. I can only imagine how I'd feel if the body under the water was my own cousin.

I silently say a quick prayer of healing for him, then turn back to the job at hand. The riverbank is a buzz of activity as the techs work the scene, their white jumpsuits bright in the late-night moonlight.

I search the faces for the one I truly hope to see. I spot Michelle coming down the bank from the bridge. She slides a few inches, then regains her footing. I hurry over to help her down to the scene, steadying her by holding her hand.

Her skin is chilled by the night air and her fingers feel tiny in mine.

"Thank you," she says, breathless after her slide. "That's a steep bank."

"I almost slid down too," I say to put her at ease. "Luckily, no one saw. I'm quite graceful," I tease.

Her hand is still in mine, and she makes no move to pull it

away. Her fingers tighten against my palm, and I feel a warmth climb up my arm.

For a moment, we are the only ones on the river, alone with the water.

"Michelle, over here," one of the techs call, ruining the moment.

She quickly drops my hand, gives me a small smile that melts my heart, then goes to work.

I watch her walk away, conscious of how her hips sway, even hidden beneath her white jumpsuit.

We've only seen each other once outside of a crime scene. An all-too-short coffee date. As soon as I get a chance, as soon as this case is wrapped up, I'm going to ask her out on a real date.

But for now, I need to focus on a different young woman. The one shoved under the branches in the river.

My heart sinks, the moment of enjoyment gone.

Marrero shines his light into the water, getting a good look at Mackenzie Odell. A small twitch of sorrow crosses his face. In the dark, I'm not sure I saw it. The man is usually as stoic as stone. I've often wondered if he has feelings for the victims he studies.

That twitch of actual human emotion makes me like the man a little. Or at least dislike him less.

I stand next to him on the bank. "Preliminary observations?" I ask.

He glances up at me, then straightens, pushing his hands against his knees. I hear the creak of age as he stands up. A creak I've been hearing in my own knees lately.

"Definitely murder," he says. "Even from here, I can see the marks on her neck. And while it's possible she floated into these branches, it's much more likely she was placed here under the bridge. The killer probably figured no one would find her."

Marrero looks around the area, then steps back and looks up to the bridge. "How was she found, exactly?"

I'd hoped he wouldn't ask. "A ghost told Rylan Flynn that she was down here," I say, bracing for his reaction.

"Sure. A ghost," he says sarcastically. "Aren't you worried about the number of dead bodies that woman has happened to find?"

I'm not surprised by his question. He's made it no secret that he doesn't like Rylan. But she's my friend and I won't talk bad about her. "She's been very helpful. Mackenzie Odell is probably pretty happy that Rylan found her right now."

Marrero's eyes narrow. "This poor woman is dead. She can't be happy about anything. I don't believe in all this ghost garbage."

"What do you believe in?" I didn't mean to ask that out loud, but I can't get the words back.

Marrero's lips turn up into what might be called a smile. "Science, my boy. Science explains everything." He turns back to his team, giving the orders to remove the body from the river so he can get a better look.

It takes six people and a sheet to lift her onto the bank. Once there, Marrero looks her over closely.

"Clothes seem to be intact," he says. "Leggings are pulled up and straight. Her shirt is on. Doesn't look like she was undressed." He lifts up the hem of her T-shirt with a gloved finger and looks under. "Her bra is in place." He sits back on his heels. "I won't know for sure until I get her back to the lab, but I'd say no sexual assault."

That was my conclusion too, but I'm glad to have it seconded.

"Strange she's missing her shoes and socks," Marrero continues. "Did she take them off? Or was she not wearing any when she was abducted?"

"Maybe she was at home and not wearing them," I offer.

"You better find out."

I pay no attention to Marrero's grumbling and focus on Kenzie. I study her face. Her eyes are open a slit, as is her mouth. As I watch, a crab crawls out from her lips.

I jump back in surprise. "Jesus."

Marrero makes a sound that might be a chuckle.

Any decent feelings I had for the man disappear.

I look around quickly for Michelle. She's bent over, looking at the ground a few paces away. She didn't see my moment of fear.

The crab crawls across Kenzie's face and into her hair.

"Get that out of here," Marrero commands one of the techs. Soon, the crab is caught and thrown back into the river.

"Anything else you can tell me?" I ask Marrero.

He gives the body another quick inspection. "What's this?" he asks, pointing to a place just above the waistband of her leggings. This side has been pulled down a few inches, and a raw spot is visible on the front of her hip.

He shines a light on the injury. "I can't be sure from here, but it looks like she was cut." He points with his gloved finger. "See how the skin is missing?" We both look to the branches. "Could be from a branch," he muses. "When she was placed into the water."

"Or someone could have cut her," I offer.

"Could be." He moves the light away.

"Why cut a small piece of hip away like that?" Michelle asks, overhearing.

Marrero looks at her a beat longer than necessary. He doesn't like being questioned, even when it's for the benefit of the case. "That's for Detective Spencer to figure out," he snaps.

I don't like his tone, but he's in charge of this scene. I give Michelle a commiserating look—a small smile steals the edges of her mouth. She looks away to keep Marrero from seeing it.

He doesn't miss it, just gives me a hard look. "This is a crime scene. Not a dating game," he grumbles, then turns back to Kenzie.

A while later, I've gotten all the information I can from the scene. Marrero has loaded the body into his van and driven off. A few techs are finishing up looking for evidence, logging anything that might be of value.

The bank is littered with cans, bottles and cigarette butts. This bridge is a well-known hangout for teens during the summer months. The remains of their fun lie in the weeds and mud. Probably just trash, but each item might be something useful to the investigation.

I scan the riverbanks as the sun begins peeking between the trees. My shoulders ache, the few hours of sleep I got before the call came in not nearly enough. The last of the techs are finishing up their work. Besides the teenage trash, there isn't much to go on.

The responsibility of the case lies heavily, drags on my heart.

I feel a bit lost without a partner to share the burden with, but Ford has his own burden.

As I watch the river slowly roll by, I take a deep breath.

I owe this to Ford and his family. I can't drop the ball.

I feel a hand on my shoulder and turn around quickly.

It's Michelle. "Hi. I didn't mean to startle you. I just wanted to tell you that we're wrapping up our search. We didn't find anything of note. My guess is that she was tossed over from the bridge and the branches caught her."

"Yeah, my thought too." I look up to the bridge. "But why this bridge?"

"It's pretty remote. The killer probably thought she'd wash away."

"Where does this river lead? Into Ashby or away?" I ask, trying to get my bearings.

"Away, I think," Michelle says. "I think it makes a turn just ahead, then runs south."

I look in that direction. "I think you're right. Nothing but farmland that way."

"And not many bridges," Michelle adds.

As the other techs trudge up the bank to the bridge, Michelle and I find ourselves alone.

I grow nervous and search for something to say. When I glance at her, the morning sun is shining on the wisps of blond hair that have come loose from her paper hat.

Even in her white jumpsuit she looks beautiful.

"I guess I should be going." She walks toward the bank. "What's your next step in the investigation?"

"I need to talk to her family and tell them what happened. I did a search earlier and her mother lives in Fort Wayne. Looks like I'm taking a little drive."

I want to ask her to come with me, but that's not possible. "I'm headed back to the lab to turn in what we found. Not that there's anything useful."

"Thank you for working tonight," I say as I follow her up the bank. I help her onto the bridge, and she takes my hand.

"My pleasure," she says once we're back on the solid concrete of the bridge.

One of the techs standing by the van calls to her. "Gotta go," she says. "Good luck with the investigation. Keep me posted, will you?"

"Sure will." I grasp the excuse to call her.

"Good luck in Fort Wayne. I'm glad I don't have to tell a mother this horrible news."

A sadness falls over the bridge.

"It's never easy. But Julia Odell deserves to hear it from me in person."

After a moment of hesitation, and another call from her colleague, she hurries away with a little wave.

I watch the crime-scene van pull away and realize I'm the last one on scene. The early light makes the bridge seem a lovely spot, not the site of a murder.

With my feet dragging, I make my way to the side of the road where my car is parked. Alone, I head toward Fort Wayne, and a mother whose world is about to be turned upside down.

I wish Ford was with me. It might make this bearable.

SIX

RYLAN FLYNN

A quick Google search and I find Julia's address in Fort Wayne. According to the internet, she lives just south of downtown. I rarely get to Fort Wayne. Ashby has all I need, and I don't like cities in general. As buildings begin to rise up from the fields, I start to get anxious. The traffic grows thicker as rush hour fills the streets. We get off the interstate and head downtown.

There are so many people, so many buildings. My back begins tingling.

There are too many ghosts.

I shift in my seat, and Ford sees.

"You okay?"

"There's a lot of people around. A lot of people means a lot of spirits."

"I hadn't thought of that. Is that why you rarely leave Ashby?" His concern sounds genuine.

"It's one of the reasons." I look out the window, wondering if the people I see on the streets are really there or just ghosts. As the high-rises of downtown crowd us, the tingle grows uncomfortable. There's just too much history around me.

"Do you want me to turn around? I can take you back home and come by myself."

I shift again, trying to make the tingle in my back stop. "No. I'll be okay. Just get through downtown and maybe it will go away."

Fort Wayne's downtown district is luckily not too large. We're soon in a more residential neighborhood. It doesn't help as much as I hoped. The old houses are full of their own energy. I start to feel surrounded—my anxiety climbs.

We finally turn down a side street, the tingles are a little less intense. Ford stops in front of a two-story house almost identical to all the other houses on the street.

"This is it," he says with trepidation.

I look around. A woman waits on the neighbor's porch, a halo of light around her.

Ford follows my gaze to the porch, which must seem empty to him.

"Is there one over there?"

"Yeah." I focus on Julia's house. "Let's just get this over."

As we get out of the car, Ford notices the vehicle we're parked in front of. "Uh-oh, that's Tyler's car," he says.

"Is he going to be mad we're here?"

"Probably. Let's find out."

I try to keep my eyes on Ford's back as we walk up the sidewalk toward Julia's house, but the spirit at the neighbor's watches with interest. I wave at her and she jumps back in surprise.

I don't have time to wonder about the ghost as we climb the steps to the porch. A cat sits on the railing at the end of it, staring at us in a bored manner. It's black, like the cat that recently decided to live in my house. I've fed the cat, and cleaned the litter box, but besides that, we're just living in the same house. This cat gives me as much attention as the one at home. None.

Before Ford can knock, the door opens and Tyler steps out.

"I'll be in touch," he says to the woman just inside. He stops short when he sees us. "What are you guys doing here?"

"We came to talk to Kenzie's mom," Ford says.

Julia Odell steps out onto the porch. "Hello? Can I help you?" Her eyes are red and her face is tear-stained.

"Mrs. Odell, I am so sorry for your loss. I'm Ford Pierce. Owen is married to my aunt. I'm a detective in Ashby," Ford says as Tyler looks on disapprovingly.

"You're not supposed to be here," Tyler says in a low voice.

"Now isn't really a good time," Julia says to Ford, glancing quickly at me. "I'm sure you know about—"

"We do. And we're trying to help," Ford pushes.

"I don't understand. I thought he was the detective. You're on the case too?"

"He isn't," Tyler interjects. "He's a detective from Ashby, but he's off the case because the victim is his relative."

"The *victim* is my daughter. If these two can help catch whoever hurt her, then I want them to help," Julia says with surprising insistence.

"That's not how this works," Tyler tries, but without much conviction.

"What can I do for you—Ford is it? And who's this?"

I reach out a hand and shake hers. "I'm Rylan Flynn. I'm sort of a consultant. I'm so sorry for your loss."

"I don't think it's set in yet. My Kenzie can't be gone. I'm sure it's a big misunderstanding," she says vaguely, sitting on a porch chair.

"I'd love to tell you that's true, but I identified her myself," Ford says gently.

Julia studies his face. "I still don't believe it," she says, taking a deep breath. "What can I do for you? I already told the detective I have no idea who would want to hurt Kenzie. She's always been a bit of a handful, maybe a few questionable friends, but nothing that would get her hurt."

"Has she been hanging out with anyone new lately?" Ford asks. "I heard she'd gotten sort of secretive."

"She's twenty now. That age, they stop telling their moms things, you know," Julia says. "Sure, she had her own life, but I didn't see anything alarming. Truly, she was doing better. In the past, she had a bit of trouble. Dropped out of school, that sort of thing. She'd turned herself around recently. Even started dressing nicer."

"Grandma Delia said she wasn't wearing makeup the last time she saw her," Ford says.

"Oh, that. Yeah, she dropped the dark look. That's what I mean. It seems she's turning a corner."

"Any reason why?" I ask.

Julia glances at me, thinking. "Probably the new guy she's seeing."

Ford and Tyler both perk up at that.

"A new boyfriend? You didn't mention that before," Tyler says.

"I forgot. I really didn't think much of it. She met him a few weeks ago. I didn't expect it to last."

"Why not?" Ford asks.

Julia studies the floorboards of the porch. "He isn't her type," she hedges.

"How so?" Tyler pushes.

"He's not from here. Or even from Ashby. I'm sure he has nothing to do with this."

"Do you know his name?" Ford asks.

"Eli Graber," Julia says, letting the name sink in.

Ford and Tyler exchange glances. "Graber? As in the furniture company?"

"I think so."

They're all so serious, I'm confused. "What's wrong with that?"

"The Grabers are well known. They're a huge, important family," Tyler says.

"So?" I still don't understand.

"They're Amish," Ford says.

"It was almost romantic. Though of course it was doomed," Julia says.

"Why doomed?" I ask.

"Amish men don't date English women," Ford explains. "It just isn't done."

"Who says?" I push.

"It's against their religion," Tyler says. "That means we have a suspect. Several of them, if his family knew."

"You're sure Kenzie was dating this Eli?" Ford asks.

"She told me herself. Said she's in love. I warned her," Julia breaks into tears. "If he hurt her, you have to catch him."

Tyler says, "We'll do our best."

"We will," Ford says at the same time.

SEVEN

RYLAN FLYNN

We leave a broken Julia on her front porch. We all hate to leave her alone, but before we go, she calls her sister, who promises to come right over. This makes me feel a little better that she won't be alone.

Tyler leads us to the cars, then turns on us.

"As much as I want this case closed, you know you can't be talking to the family of the victim," he says to Ford.

"This is my family."

"Exactly the point. Please, I don't like it either, but there's a protocol to follow." He looks at his shoes. "Chief McKay called a little while ago and he's partnering me up with Faith Hudson on this one."

Ford nods thoughtfully, but his shoulders tense. "Hudson's a good officer. I know she's had her eye on a detective spot. She just moved here from Indianapolis, right? You think she can handle it?"

Tyler looks uncomfortable. "I guess she'll have to. This is too big to mess up. Besides, she was a detective in Indy. I heard she only took the officer job because she had to. Recently divorced and moved back home. I'm sure she'll work out fine."

"Maybe if I talk to McKay, he'll relent and let me back on."

"I don't think so," Tyler says. "He was pretty adamant when I talked to him. I won't tell him you two were here this morning. Just stay out of the way and let me and Faith handle this."

While they're talking, I've been watching the ghost on the neighbor's porch. She seems very interested in us. She descends the steps, then crosses the yard to the sidewalk.

She gets very close to my face.

"You can see me, can't you?" she asks.

I try to ignore her, to follow the conversation.

She waves a hand in front of my face. "Please don't do that," I whisper.

Ford studies me. "A ghost?"

"She's from the neighbor's house. She's right here."

"Talk to me. No one talks to me. I've been trying to get Mandy's attention, but she won't listen."

"Just a second. She's very persistent," I tell Ford and Tyler. "What do you want to say to Mandy?" I ask the woman, stepping away from the men.

"I knew you could hear me. I knew it! You need to help me out. Mandy and Eddie live in my house. I've been trying to tell Mandy that Eddie's girlfriend has been coming over while she's at work."

"That's terrible," I say.

"I know. I don't know what she sees in him. As far as I can tell, she has no idea. I need to warn her."

"Why are you so interested?" I ask, stepping off the sidewalk, following her toward the house.

"I know a thing or two about Eddie and his cheating ways."

She rubs her neck, and I see the marks there, the finger-shaped bruises.

"He strangled you and you've been here ever since?"

"Yes. I dated Eddie a few years ago, but I caught him cheating. Walked in on him right in our bedroom upstairs there. He got so mad. I have to warn Mandy. I'm worried he'll do the same thing to her."

"What do you want me to do?"

"Tell her. She's home right now." She starts leading up the walk. "Come on."

"I can't just go tell her a ghost says your husband is cheating on you."

"They aren't married. They're engaged, though. Wedding is a few months away. I can't let her make that mistake. I'm telling you, he's dangerous."

I look to Ford and Tyler. "I need to go tell someone their fiancé is cheating on them. I'll be right back."

"Good luck," Ford says. I love that he doesn't question the outlandish statement.

I follow the ghost to the house—she waits while I knock. A moment later, a young woman opens the door.

"That's her. Tell her," the ghost says.

"Are you Mandy?" I ask.

"Yes," she says warily. "What can I do for you? It's very early." She seems less than pleased to see me on her doorstep. I'm about to ruin her day.

"Tell her. Tell her," the ghost demands.

"I'm really sorry to have to tell you, but Eddie is cheating on you," I blurt out, not sure how else to explain.

Mandy's face grows pale, then she flushes with anger. "How dare you come here to my door and say such lies? Eddie wouldn't do that."

"I know it's hard to hear, but it's true. She comes over when you're at work."

"Tell her it's Monica. Monica with the big hair," the ghost prompts.

"You're a liar," Mandy says, and tries to shut the door. I put my foot in the jamb.

"It's Monica. Monica with the big hair."

Mandy freezes. "My friend, Monica?"

I look to the ghost for confirmation. She nods.

"Yes. Your friend. I'm so sorry."

Mandy crumples. "How do you know this?"

I debate telling her the truth, then ask, "Do you believe in ghosts?"

Now she looks angry. "I do, but what's that have to do with Eddie?"

"Your house has a ghost," I say. Mandy tries to shut the door again, but my foot is still in the way.

"You're a crazy person. Get off my porch."

"Tell her about the lights. I flick them all the time," the ghost says.

"Do your lights flicker?"

"So? It's an old house."

"And the water. I turn it on," the ghost says.

"And the water turns on by itself?"

"How do you know all this? Have you been spying on me?" Mandy demands.

"You have a ghost. Her name is..."

"Fiona. My name is Fiona. I've been here for, what year is it?" the ghost asks.

"Her name is Fiona, and she's been here for years. She's the one that told me about Eddie and Monica. Fiona's right here with us."

"Who are you?" Mandy asks in blatant disbelief.

"I'm Rylan Flynn. I work with ghosts. I can see and talk to them. Fiona stopped me on the sidewalk and wanted to help you."

"You're telling me a ghost is on my porch and she's seen Eddie with Monica? She wants to help me?"

"I don't want her to marry him," Fiona says. "Or even be near him."

"She doesn't want you to get married to a cheater." I

swallow hard. "Or a murderer."

"A what?"

"Eddie killed her a few years ago. She caught him cheating and he strangled her."

"That can't be true."

"I see the marks on her neck."

"Why does she care? I don't know her," Mandy says, rubbing her own neck.

"She knows you. She lives here with you. She's been trying to get your attention for a while now."

Mandy rubs her upper arms. "A ghost? Right here? And Eddie's cheating on me? And murdered someone?"

Mandy stares into the distance a moment, then seems to come to a conclusion. "You know, I kind of wondered about Eddie cheating. Once in a while, things just seemed off. When I asked, he told me I was crazy." Her voice trails off.

"Has he ever hurt you?" I ask.

Her expression clouds as she rubs her upper arms. "That's none of your business."

"I'm sorry this is happening to you."

Her head snaps up in a rush of determination. "Me too. But he's going to be even sorrier. Now if you'll excuse me, I'm calling my brother to help me pack my things."

Mandy retreats into the house.

"Yes!" Fiona yelps and gives a little jump. "We did it. I've been trying to get her attention for months now."

"You helped her. Maybe even saved her life."

"Now what? Can I come with you? I'm tired of hanging out in this house all the time. Bad enough I lived here when I was alive. It was rough here with Eddie. This afterlife thing hasn't been fun either. I keep replaying my murder, wishing I had been able to get away. They never caught him, you know. No one knows what happened to me. He threw me in a dumpster and that was that."

"That's so tragic."

"At least I can spare Mandy a similar fate."

On the far end of the porch, I see the familiar light, the door to the other side.

"You've done what you were still here for. You can cross now," I say somberly. "The light is behind you."

Fiona looks over her shoulder and sees the light. "You mean I can go to heaven? I can see my grandma again?"

"You can. Just step into it. I'll say a prayer for you."

She smiles and hurries across the porch toward the light as I begin praying out loud.

"Thank you," she says, then steps into the light without a backward glance.

The light disappears and Fiona is gone.

Only then do I notice Ford standing at the foot of the steps. "I heard you praying and wanted to offer my support. Did the ghost cross over?"

"She did. We warned Mandy that her fiancé was dangerous. She's leaving him with her brother's help." I walk down the steps and into his arms, leaning my cheek against his shoulder. "Fiona was murdered here in the past by this Eddie guy. Can you look into it?"

"I'll do my best," Ford says.

"I'm ready to go home. I'm really tired." I've been up over twenty-four hours and had two ghost encounters, plus all the spirit energy in the city. I'm wiped out.

He kisses the top of my head. I lean back and look up at him. "Aren't you worried Tyler will see?"

"Nope. I told him about us just now. He couldn't be happier."

Tyler waves sheepishly when I look toward the cars.

"Can we go back to Ashby now?"

EIGHT

RYLAN FLYNN

Ford and I travel silently through downtown Fort Wayne. I don't feel well. My back tingles like crazy and I'm thoroughly exhausted. By the time we cross the Maumee River and the old fort, I have to squeeze my eyes shut to block out the sprits.

"That bad?" he asks.

"Luckily the fort is just a replica, but this area is steeped in history."

When I venture to open my eyes, I see a ghost in the middle of the road, dressed in a Revolutionary-period uniform.

Our car passes right through him.

I flinch and look over my shoulder out the back window. The ghost doesn't seem to have noticed us.

"What is it?" Ford asks.

"Nothing." I turn back toward the front as we take the curves that lead us past the mall. The tingles in my back grow a little less as we head out of town. I relax against the seat, barely able to keep my head up.

"I hate to ask, but when we get back to town, can you take me home? I'm not used to being up for more than a day, and all this ghost activity is wearing me out."

"Of course. Just lay your head back and we'll be home soon."

I do as he says and soon drift off.

When I open my eyes again, we're pulling into my driveway.

I yawn and sit up, but I have a hard time waking. I shake my head to clear it.

"Go get some rest," Ford says.

"What are you going to do?"

"Tyler made it pretty clear he didn't want me anywhere near this case. I think, for now, my best plan is to be with my family. My mom texted me while you were asleep. Everyone is over at Aunt Tammy's. I should be with them."

"That's a good idea."

He leans across the center console and kisses me on the cheek. "You rest and I'll call you later."

"Okay." I wish there was something I could say to take away the pain in his eyes. We're silent a beat, then I say, "I'm so sorry you're going through this."

"Me too."

I open my door, then wave goodbye. As I watch him drive off, a deep sadness fills me. I'd like to say I don't know what it's like to lose a family member to murder.

Unfortunately, I know the pain all too well—this whole case is pulling up memories I don't want to have.

I walk around to the back of the house and let myself into the overcrowded dining room through the sliding patio door. I've managed to keep this door accessible, even if the front door is blocked. The piles of boxes and stacks of furniture surround me, pressing in on me.

The hoarded house is at once soothing and oppressive. I take a moment to let it all sink in. Piles loom in the dim light, stacks of boxes leaning dangerously.

A blur of black shoots across the room toward my feet.

I squeal and step back in fear, before I realize it's just the cat that decided to live here. He looks up and meows loudly.

"You hungry?" I cross into the kitchen and the bag of cat food. I fill a bowl, then check his water. He munches, making soft noises.

"I really should name you if you're going to stay here," I say. "You're a pretty black color... What about Onyx?"

The cat stops eating and looks up.

"You like that? Onyx? That's a black rock. It fits you."

Onyx goes back to his food.

From down the hall, the ghost of my murdered mom calls, "Rylan? Are you home?"

"I'm here, Mom. Just got in."

I follow the path to the hall and soon find Mom sitting on her bed.

"Hey," I say, leaning against the doorframe.

"You didn't come home last night. I was worried."

Sometimes, Mom has no concept of time or where she is. This must be a good day.

"I was working," I hedge. I don't want to ruin this clear time with tragedy.

"On your show with Mickey?"

"Yes, sort of. That's what I was doing, but then I was with Ford."

She studies my face, and I feel my cheeks grow warm. "With Ford. On a case?"

"Yeah. Something like that." I walk into the room. I don't want to get into this with her right now. I want to enjoy her being here still. Kenzie's family doesn't have that luxury.

I sink onto the bed. "I love you, Mom," I say sincerely. "I probably didn't say it enough before, but I'm saying it now."

She reaches for my cheek and my skin grows cold. Her expression turns sour—she reaches again, her hand going through my face.

"What?" she asks. She does it again.

I pull back. Having a ghost go through you is not comfortable.

Her eyes cloud over and she loses interest. She picks up her brush and runs it over her hair, over the hole in her head.

I sigh deeply, sad to see her go.

"I'm going to get some sleep." I stand and head for the door.

"Okay, dear," she calls absently. In the doorway, I look back. Am I doing the right thing by keeping her here on this side? I could help her cross over.

"Not today," I mutter, not ready to say goodbye for real.

I scoot past the pile of boxes in front of the door to my brother Keaton's childhood room. I'm careful not to touch them, to disturb the thing behind the door. I make it to my room safely. The giant blue teddy bear I recently acquired from a garage sale sits on my bed where I left him.

Ford named him Darby. As long as Darby stays put, he's a great comfort to me. Lately, he's taken to moving around the house while I'm gone.

After changing my clothes and climbing into bed, I curl around Darby. Onyx soon joins me and purrs loudly from the foot of the bed.

I'm as content as I can be under the circumstances.

The thing down the hall is quiet.

I'm nearly asleep when Darby shifts in my arms.

"I love you," a small child's voice says.

My eyes fly open, and Onyx jumps off the bed, his back arched.

I'm still holding Darby, and he wriggles from my hands, falling on the floor. He lands on his back, his baby blue arms reaching for me, his sewn-on smile mocking me.

"I love you," the voice repeats, coming from the bear.

I shove against the wall next to the bed, as far from Darby as I can get.

"Who's there?" I shout. My back tingles almost painfully.

Darby's arms move up and down.

I shout out in surprise and Onyx hisses at the toy.

I demand, "What do you want?"

Darby's eyes are blank, his arms still.

He's just a bear full of stuffing. When the initial shock wears off, I pick him up with the tips of my fingers on his paw. Holding him in front of me, I carry him to the front room. Once there, I toss him as far into the piles of stuff as I can. I wait, breathing heavily.

When I'm sure Darby won't talk again, I go back to bed.

Even with Onyx curled up at the foot of my bed, it takes a long time for my heart to stop pounding and sleep to come.

NINE

RYLAN FLYNN

I'm still shaken by Darby speaking to me. Even in my world, stuffed animals don't move and speak. I shake my head, turning my attention to Ford. I glance across the car as we drive out of Ashby toward the Amish area. The pale blue T-shirt and leather jacket he wears this afternoon suit him. I can't seem to keep my eyes off him.

He catches me looking.

"What?" he asks.

"I rarely see you out of uniform. It looks good on you." The words feel both foreign and fitting on my tongue. I wonder how long it will take to get used to being honest about my feelings for him.

"You look pretty good yourself." He reaches across the center console and takes my hand. We drive like this for a while, out of Ashby and north. As the fields take over the landscape, I can't help wondering about Kenzie dating a young Amish man.

"What I don't get," I say, breaking the companionable silence, "is Eli Graber must only have a horse and buggy. How did he get to see Kenzie without a car?"

"It's only a few miles, really."

"Which is easy with a car, not in a buggy. It's not like he could drive up to her apartment."

"Kenzie has a car. I understand it's back at her place. Besides, lots of Amish get rides into town."

I think on this a while, chewing my lower lip.

"Stop that," he teases.

"Stop what?"

"Chewing on your lip. It makes me want to kiss you."

I break into a wide smile, amazed all over again at where our relationship has taken us. Is it okay to talk about kissing right now?

If it helps Ford cope, then that's good.

"Sorry. I was just thinking," I say. "Even if Kenzie had a car, did she just drive up to his farm and pick him up? I don't see that happening. From what I understand, the Amish don't like strangers too much. Especially ones dating their sons."

"What are you getting at?"

"Where did they meet up? What did they do? Did she take him to the bridge? That's an out-of-the-way place."

Ahead on the road, a horse and buggy comes into view, the horse's legs swinging rhythmically. Ford slows down and passes.

Amish farms now dot the fields. Barns and large, simple houses. I can tell the Amish houses from the English ones because they don't have power lines running to them.

Each farm is clean and organized. Horses in many of the pastures. It's lovely.

Ford checks the GPS and says, "I think this is it." He slows in front of a wide white house with a group of barns off to the left. He turns down the long drive. The horses in the pasture lift their heads as we go by.

I grow nervous as we approach the house. The Amish are very devout. I don't know their exact feelings on ghosts and the other world, but I doubt they'll take to me if they know what I do.

"Maybe it wasn't a good idea bringing me with you." I rub the knees of my jeans, wishing I'd chosen a pair that didn't have holes torn fashionably into them. Amish women wear long dresses, they do not show their legs like this.

"Why's that?"

"What if they find out about me seeing ghosts? They'll probably toss me off the property, or worse."

"So don't tell them." He makes it sound so simple.

"But my back is tingling."

He grows serious. "Where is it?"

I shift, the tingle becoming uncomfortable. "I'm not sure yet."

A woman in bare feet, wearing a pale blue dress that nearly reaches the ground, comes outside and eyes us with a mixture of curiosity and defensiveness.

"Let's just see how this goes," Ford soothes. "I don't think Eli is here. Or any man for that matter. If there was, they'd be out by now. That must be Eli's mom."

The woman's face turns even more guarded as we approach her.

"Hello," Ford says as pleasantly as he can.

"Hello," she responds tentatively. "Can I help you?"

A child runs out of the house, her dress matching her mother's. The girl hides behind the woman's skirt and stares at me with open interest. I give her a shy smile and she ducks behind Mom.

"I'm Ford Pierce and this is Rylan Flynn. We're looking for Eli."

The woman crosses her arms. "I already told the others that Eli's not here. I don't know where he is."

Ford glances at me. "Was that a detective you talked to?"

"Two detectives. One was a woman."

"That must be Tyler and Faith Hudson," he says to me.

"I don't remember their names. They said some young

woman got killed in Ashby. I told them it has nothing to do with us. Especially not with Eli." The woman lifts her chin.

"The woman's name is Mackenzie Odell. Does that sound familiar?"

Something in her eyes flickers, then they grow cold again. "Never heard of her."

"She goes by Kenzie," I offer.

The door opens again and a young woman in a pale tan dress joins us. "Everything okay?"

"Yes, Hannah. These people were just leaving."

"Have you ever heard Eli mention a woman named Kenzie?" Ford asks Hannah. "She was murdered, we found her body last night. We understand the two of them were dating."

Hannah looks to her mother for guidance. "I... don't think so," she says hesitantly.

"It's important that we know the truth," Ford says, using his cop voice. Hannah jumps a little at the sharp tone. "Kenzie is dead, and Eli may be involved."

"There's no way Eli is involved in anything like that," the mother says. "Now, if you don't mind, please leave."

The little girl peeks around her mother's hip, and the mother pushes her back as if to protect her from us.

The whole time we've been talking, the tingle in my back has been gnawing at me. I look around the farm and see what's triggering it.

A bearded man in dark clothes and a dark hat walks from the barn toward us. He has a shimmer around him.

"You get out of here!" he shouts at us, waving his arms.

I stare directly at the ghost and shake my head a little. He freezes in mid-wave, his arms over his head.

"You can see me?" he asks.

I nod as imperceptibly as I can, while I turn to follow Ford back to the car.

The man hurries to my side. "What do you want here? You upset Ruth and Hannah."

With my back to the others, walking slowly, I ask the ghost, "What do you know about Eli dating Kenzie Odell?"

"I heard those others talking about it. She was murdered. I warned Eli that nothing good would come of him dating an English woman. He, of course, couldn't hear me. But Eli didn't hurt that girl. He's not the type."

"We're trying to help him," I say, to put the man at ease. "We need to talk to him. Where is Eli now?" I ask as I reach the car.

The man takes off his hat, turning it in his hands, thinking. He seems to make a decision and puts his hat back on.

"Making a delivery to the grocery store in Wolcottville. That's where he met that girl."

"How do you know all this?"

"I've been on this farm for a long time. First when I lived here with my family, and now like this."

"What happened?" I ask gently.

"A horse kicked me," he says simply. "Right in the head." He rubs the back of his head. When he turns, I see the bloody indent from the hoof.

"I'm so sorry," I say earnestly. "How do you know Eli was with Kenzie?"

"I overheard him telling Ruth about her. Don't fall for her innocent act. She knows all about what that boy was up to."

I look back toward the mother, who now stands in the door, watching to be sure we leave. The daughters have already gone inside.

"Why did she lie?"

"Why do all mothers lie? To protect their children. Ruth isn't going to talk. I'm sorry about what happened to the girl, but you two are wasting your time looking at Eli."

"We still need to talk to him," I say. "But thank you for the information."

Ruth is still watching from the door.

"You better go," the ghost says. "I don't like you upsetting her."

I nod to Ford, and we climb back into the car.

"Who was it this time?"

"An Amish man. He said Ruth knows all about Eli and Kenzie. He overheard them talking about it. She's lying to protect her son."

"Where is Eli now?"

"At the grocery in Wolcottville, making a delivery."

Ford puts the car into drive and makes a three-point turn. "Let's go shopping."

TEN

RYLAN FLYNN

The Amish grocery looks more like a long barn than a store. I remember coming here a few times with Dad when I was a kid. Dad raved about the fresh-baked bread and farm-fresh eggs. I remember the candy. Bins full of single pieces took up an entire wall. You got to pick out your favorites and pay by the pound.

"Think they still have the candy?" I ask Ford as he parks the car.

"Oh, yeah. I remember that. I loved the Bit-O-Honey."

"Me too!"

Ford locks his eyes with mine. "I'm glad you're here," he says. "You make all this bearable."

I touch his hand. "I'm glad I'm here too."

At the far end of the building there's an open buggy backed to a loading door. A young man dressed in a plain blue shirt and dark pants is unloading bread.

"That must be him," Ford says. "How do we want to play this?"

"Maybe I should talk to him by myself. You're a bit intimidating."

"I am not."

"Trust me, you are. I might be able to get something out of him." I watch Eli lifting stacks of bread. "I wonder if he knows about Kenzie yet."

"I doubt it. You sure you don't want me to talk to him? You've never given a death notice on your own before."

I open the car door before I can change my mind. "I'll be fine. Wish me luck."

I crunch across the gravel parking lot, past a row of horses and buggies tied to a wooden rail.

The man I think is Eli doesn't pay me any attention until I'm right next to him. Even then, he barely looks my way. "No pictures, please," he grumbles.

"I don't want to take your picture," I say, a bit confused.

"Sorry," he lifts some bread out of the buggy. "I thought you were a tourist."

"My name is Rylan. Are you Eli Graber?"

He pauses in his unloading. "Why?"

"I want to ask you about Kenzie Odell."

His eyes widen in surprise, but then he recovers. "I don't know her." He turns back to the bread, picking up a loaf.

"Her mom told us you two were dating."

He stops, stands up tall and imposing. "What do you want?"

"I need to tell you about Kenzie," I stall, studying the buggy's wheel instead of his face.

He's suddenly concerned. "Tell me what? All right, I know her. I haven't been able to get ahold of her for two days. That's not like her."

My mouth goes dry—my tongue doesn't want to say the words. The memory of Kenzie's parents getting the news is fresh in my mind. I'm about to ruin this man's life.

When I don't answer right away, he pushes. "Did something bad happen?"

"I'm so sorry. She was found murdered early this morning."

He stiffens. "Murdered? That can't be right."

"I saw her myself. I'm so sorry."

He tosses the bread back into the buggy. "I don't understand. How did this happen? Who did it?"

"We don't know."

He glances over my leather jacket and torn skinny jeans. "You're obviously not police. Why aren't they here telling me? Who are you?"

"My name is Rylan. I'm helping the police. Well, sort of. I'm the one that found Kenzie. She was under the bridge on Ostermeyer Road. Does that location mean anything to you?"

"Never heard of it." He pulls off his dark hat and rubs his hair. "You're kidding, right? Kenzie just hasn't answered her phone. That's all."

"Do you often call her? How does that work?"

"My friend has a cell phone. When I can, I call her. She drives up here and we meet at the historic park where that author lived years ago."

"Gene Stratton Porter?"

"Yes. It's way off the road, no one goes there at night."

"Your mom doesn't mind you dating an English woman?"

His eyes grow even larger. "How do you know about my mother? Did she tell you about Kenzie and me?"

"No, her mom told us about you. I'm just guessing your mom knew too. Mothers usually do," I hedge.

"I had to tell her. Mother and I are very close." He runs his fingers around the rim of his hat. "You can't tell anyone else about us. I could get into trouble. Especially with Father and Grandfather Elisha. They will be so mad."

"You sure they don't know already?"

"I'm pretty sure," he answers without conviction.

"You couldn't keep her a secret forever. What was your plan?"

"I don't know. I just—Kenzie was so different. I met her here. She saw me delivering the bread and she started asking me questions. Not like the tourists do, but like she was honestly interested in me. Not what I am, but who I am." He looks to the sky and swallows hard. "She can't really be gone," he chokes.

I'm touched by his emotional display. I wonder if it's real— or forced for my benefit. I can't quite get a read on him.

"I know this is difficult, but I need to ask. Were you with her two nights ago, the night she disappeared?"

"No. I was not." His voice breaks a little and his eyes grow red and damp.

I'm surprised again at this display. Aren't the Amish usually stoic to a fault?

"Do you know who would hurt her?" I push. "Did she have any enemies, anyone that was bothering her?"

"No. Not that I can think of. She didn't have many friends. At least not that she talked about. Just Meera, really."

"Meera?"

"Meera Sharma. They were high school friends, and the only one Kenzie still saw, or at least that she told me about."

"We'll need to talk to her." I try another tactic. "I heard she got into trouble and had to drop out of college. Do you know why?"

"She didn't tell me. She rarely talked about her past. I got the feeling she was hiding something, but I never pushed it."

"Is there anything you can tell me? Anything that could help find the person who did this?" I try to keep the frustration out of my voice but fail.

"Look, I love Kenzie, but she didn't tell me about her past. I'm sorry I can't be more help, but I'm reeling here. I can't believe she's gone."

He wipes at his eyes angrily.

I try a more gentle approach. "Anything that sticks out as unusual? The tiniest thing could be a clue to what happened."

"She had an odd tattoo. Does that count?"

"Depends. What was it of?"

"Just numbers. One, seven, zero, six, two, one. It was on her hip. I asked her about it, and she got really defensive. She said she was drunk when she got it and it didn't mean anything. She also had a butterfly tattoo on her shoulder. A monarch I think. She always seemed ashamed of them."

"Anything else? Anything at all?" I keep pushing.

"Just that I love her." He swallows hard. "She was different than the girls I know. She was a lot darker when we met. Lots of makeup and dark clothes. But she'd changed with me. Started dressing more plain. Stopped wearing makeup and jewelry. I wondered if she would convert and we could get married. Not soon, but maybe someday." His voice trails off and he looks away.

Is he acting? Or are his feelings real? I wish Ford had come to talk to him. He's better at reading people than I am. Of course, Eli probably wouldn't be so open with Ford here.

He picks up some bread and turns brusque. "I have to finish unloading this. I'm sorry I can't help you more." He turns his back on me. "I have nothing left to say."

"You going to be okay?" I ask, full of concern despite my suspicions.

"I have to be. It's bad enough that my mother knows about the relationship. I can't let on that anything bad has happened, or father and grandfather will find out."

"Is that so bad?"

He turns and looks me directly in the eye. "I'm the oldest son of Aaron Graber. I'm the oldest grandson of Elisha Graber. In our world, that means something."

"Are you set to take over the furniture business?"

"Eventually. I've worked there for years. This delivery job is just on the side, a way to get out a bit. And it brought me Kenzie, for however short a time I got to know her."

I don't know how to respond to this. The young man is under a lot of family pressure. Is it enough to kill for? I'm not going to get anymore answers, so I say goodbye and leave him to the bread.

When I return to the car and Ford, I tell him everything Eli said, including her school friend, Meera, and the odd number tattoo, 170621.

"Do you think he did it?" he asks.

"I'm certain of only one thing. Eli's life will never be the same."

ELEVEN

RYLAN FLYNN

The drive back to Ashby is too short. I've never spent so many hours alone with Ford. A tiny part of me had wondered if I would get tired of being with him. Dreaming of being with him and the reality of his presence are two different things.

I needn't have worried. As we pull into my driveway, I feel a sense of loss, and I'm not even out of the car yet.

He puts the car in park, then turns in his seat to face me. The sun is setting behind him, darkening his face into shadow.

"This was quite a day," he says. He sounds tired, and I remember he didn't get the nap I did. He only got a few hours of sleep in before I called him about Kenzie.

"It sure was." Nerves jump in my belly. Do I invite him in? Am I ready for him to see the house? Am I ready for what might come next?

I try to imagine him in my room, in my bed, covered with pillows and stuffed animals.

I can't picture it.

Then I remember Darby and how he talked last night.

"Do you remember that big blue stuffed bear I have? You named him Darby?"

"Yeah. Not everyday you drive up with a huge toy."

I search his shadowed face, meet his eyes.

Can I trust him with this?

"I think there's something wrong with him." I test the waters.

"Wrong how?" He leans forward, interested.

"He's been moving around the house. I've found him in places I didn't leave him."

"You think he's haunted?" No note of sarcasm. Only concern.

"I do. This morning, he moved his arms and talked." I continue eye contact, hoping he'll believe me.

"That had to be terrifying. Even for you."

"I didn't know what to do. I finally just threw him into the front room behind some boxes and left him there."

"Have you dealt with haunted objects before?"

I think of the thing in Keaton's room. Of the shadow-filled objects the killers have all had, which I was forced to destroy. Haunted items can have a lot of power.

"No," I lie. The deception stings my conscience, but I'm not ready to tell him about all that yet. Not until I figure out what it means.

"Maybe there's a spirit stuck in the bear. That happens, doesn't it?" he asks.

"That's what I was thinking. But I don't know who it is or how to get rid of it."

"The same way you do the other spirits stuck here. This one's just stuck in a different way."

The car has grown darker as the sun dips below the horizon. "Usually, they're stuck for a reason. I can talk to them, figure out what they need and help them. How do I help a stuffed animal?"

"You said it talked. What did it say?"

"I love you."

Even in the growing dark, I can see the tiny flinch of surprise.

"That's what the bear said," I add quickly. He relaxes. "Darby said 'I love you.'"

Ford thinks a moment, his detective brain working. "Where did you get him?"

"From a garage sale over on Wilder Street."

"Do you think you'd remember the house? We could go ask the previous owner about him."

"And tell her she sold me a haunted bear? I don't think that would go over well."

"Don't tell her that. We'll just say you really like the bear and want some history on it."

I love that he's making himself part of this, offering to help. Especially with Kenzie's case to work on. "You'd go with me?"

"Of course. First thing tomorrow. Then we'll go talk to Kenzie's friend Meera. We need to give Tyler a little time to talk to her first. I don't want him running into us again. I'd like him not to know we're still asking questions for as long as possible."

"That makes sense." I glance toward the front door, still unsure how to proceed. Do I kiss him goodbye? Is that appropriate with the murder and all?

I don't have to wonder long.

"Rylan?" His voice is husky.

I shift until I'm facing him. "Yes?" My voice sounds strange, even to my own ears.

"Would it be wrong to kiss you now with everything going on?"

"I hope not." I make the decision for us and lean across until my lips touch his. The kiss is fiery and insistent. Desire floods my blood as he puts one hand in my hair, the other reaching around my waist, skimming the hem of my T-shirt.

I suddenly wish I had invited him in and that we were actually on a date, not on an investigation.

When he finally pulls away, I'm breathless and my face is warm.

"That was nice," he whispers.

"Yes, it was."

"I like this with you. Much better than fighting, like we usually do." The hand that was in my hair finds my shoulder and pulls me closer. The hand at the hem of my T-shirt finds a tiny piece of skin to rub.

Tingles snake up my back but have nothing to do with a ghost.

The center console is pushing into my hip painfully, but I don't care. I could stay like this forever. I close my eyes and lean my head on his shoulder, enjoying the moment.

His phone rings, loud in the cozy confines of the car.

I sit up reluctantly as he digs in his pocket. He glances at the screen.

"It's Chief McKay," he says with trepidation. I don't know if I should get out to give him some privacy, or stay and see what the chief has to say.

Ford grabs my hand, so I stay.

"Pierce," he answers the phone, then listens. I can't make out the words, but I can't miss the tone. McKay is angry.

Ford listens patiently until there's a break in the tirade.

"I understand," he says tightly. "I'll do my best, but this is my family we're talking about."

McKay continues, calmer now.

"Okay," Ford says, then hangs up.

"Not good?" I ask quietly.

"He found out we talked to Kenzie's mom and that we went to Wolcottville. He's not happy."

"Oh."

"He also knows you're with me." He runs a hand over the stubble on his chin. "He's pretty clear that he wants me to stay far away. I get it, I do. The case needs to be clean to stand up in court. But they don't even have a suspect besides Eli. I don't want to miss anything." He puts both hands on the steering wheel and squeezes. "I can't just sit home while my family grieves," he says quietly.

"No one can stop you from asking questions. As long as you don't break any laws, you can snoop around. What's the worst that can happen?"

"You could get hurt. We have to be careful."

"I'm not going to get hurt."

"You have in the past. I'm not sure I could take it if something happens to you again." His voice is low and full of emotion.

"I'm with you. Nothing will happen to me."

"Just promise me you'll keep it that way." He searches my eyes.

"I promise," I say. Uncomfortable, I change the subject. "So, Meera?"

He thinks for a moment, then makes a decision. "So, pick you up at nine? We'll go see about Darby, then follow up on Meera?"

"I'll be ready." I kiss him on the cheek, not wanting to start the fire again, knowing I won't be able to stop—and now is not the time.

I wait on the front walk and wave goodbye. Once he's out of sight, I walk around to the back door, not sure why I feel the need to pretend. He already knows about the stuff.

I'm smiling as I let myself into the dining room.

Darby sits on top of the pile on the table. His stitched smile seems sinister.

I make a sound of shock, my hand flying to my mouth.

"I love you," Darby says.

Onyx is under the table, hissing.

I almost turn around and leave. I could go to Mickey's for the night, or I could call Ford back.

I steel my nerves and reach for the bear. "You will not scare me out of my own house," I say too loudly.

Picking him up by the tip of an ear, I carry him to the garage and toss him out.

Onyx rubs against my ankle when I return. Feeling proud of myself, I look at the cat. "You hungry?"

TWELVE

RYLAN FLYNN

"You're sure this is the house?" Ford asks as we walk toward the front door of a small ranch.

I look around. "I'm pretty sure. There was stuff outside for the garage sale and a sign in the yard. I think I remember this gnome." I point to a statue in the front flower bed.

"Okay, then. Here goes nothing." Ford knocks on the front door. I stare at the gnome as we wait, my belly swimming with nerves.

A woman that looks vaguely familiar opens the door. "Hello?" she asks, her expression friendly.

I step forward. "Good morning, we hate to bother you, but you had a garage sale a while back."

Her face grows weary. "Is there something wrong? All sales are final at a garage sale. Everyone knows that."

"Nothing wrong. At least nothing like that," I say. "I bought a large stuffed bear at that sale."

"My daughter's bear. Yes." She seems confused.

"We just wanted a little history on the bear," Ford says. "Could we speak to your daughter?"

The woman's face crumples, then she recovers. "I... I'm

sorry, my daughter passed away a few months ago. That's why we had the sale, to help with the medical bills." She shuffles her feet uncomfortably.

"I'm so sorry," I say. "How old was she?"

"Seven," she sniffles.

"Oh my," Ford says.

"Leukemia. She battled bravely, but she lost in the end." The woman drops her eyes to the ground. "I don't understand why you're asking about Elsa. Is there a problem with her bear?"

Ford and I exchange glances.

"My name is Rylan, and this is Ford. What's your name?" I stall.

"Rochelle White." She pushes a stray strand of dark hair behind her ear.

"I—well, we—kind of study ghosts. I have a show on YouTube where we do ghost encounters."

Rochelle's eyes narrow. "Ghosts? What kind of crazy are you trying to sell here?"

"No crazy. There are actually ghosts all around," I try to explain.

"Sure there are." She grips the door and begins to shut it. "I've heard enough. First you make me think about my poor Elsa, then you bring up ghosts. You two are nuts. Get off my property." She slams the door so hard, the windows shake.

"Well, that didn't go well," I say.

"Not really," Ford agrees, stepping away from the door. "Guess you deal with skeptics a lot."

"You have no idea." As I turn, my foot slips off the walk and I lose my balance. Ford grabs my arm just in time to keep me from falling on the gnome statue.

"Careful." His hand slides down my arm, taking my hand, and he leads me back to the car.

Hand in hand under the morning sun, I can't help but smile.

"Do you think it's Elsa in the bear?" Ford asks once we're on the road again.

"I hope so. I was pretty scared when it started talking, but if Elsa is attached to the bear, she might just be trying to communicate. The ghosts I've dealt with are misunderstood, not scary really."

I think of the thing in Keaton's room and know not all spirits are friendly.

"Or it's just trying to trick you," he says seriously. "Have you worked with a haunted object before?"

"Not really," I hedge, running my hands down the legs of my skinny jeans, hoping he won't press me. "I could call my friend Lorraine. You know the White Witch? I bet she knows a thing or two about haunted objects. I could ask her what to do."

"That's a good idea. Now, what can we do with Darby in the meantime? Do you want me to take a look at him?"

"You'd do that? You're not scared?"

"Not scared, more interested. I've never seen a haunted bear before."

"You won't be able to hear him, or Elsa, or whatever's in it."

"True, but I'd like to see him anyway. Maybe I can help." I look at him in disbelief. "Besides, we're waiting for Tyler to talk to Kenzie's friend before us."

"I guess we could try. I tossed him in the garage last night. If it's Elsa in Darby, she's probably scared," I say as we pull up to my house. "Maybe I overreacted."

"Anyone would have been frightened by a stuffed bear talking and moving."

"But I'm not just anyone."

"Don't beat yourself up. We're helping her now. Maybe you can talk her out of the bear."

I look at him seriously. "Did you ever think you'd be having this conversation? It's kind of odd."

"I'm used to odd where you're concerned. I'm just happy to be helping," he says with a twinkle in his eye.

"Then let's go see him."

I open the garage door—piles of boxes from my old apartment still fill the space. "Sorry about the mess."

"No problem. Now where is he?" We search the garage, but the giant bright blue bear is not here.

"I swear I threw him in here last night," I say, confusion and worry mixing. "I can't believe this happened again."

"Has he moved through walls before?" Ford asks.

"Around the house, but not through walls." I look toward the door to the house—it's ajar a few inches. I touch the door. "I'm pretty sure I closed this. Closed it hard."

"Let's go in and find him."

Fear flushes through my veins. "Inside the house?"

Ford takes me by the shoulders, searches my face. "You're going to have to let me in sometime. I told you, I understand about the stuff. I had a great aunt that did the same thing. Her house was full of all kinds of things. As a kid, I thought it was cool. So much stuff to look at."

"It's not cool, believe me."

"Do you trust me?"

I've trusted him most of life. "Of course."

"Then trust me with this. I promise, I won't judge."

My hand rests on the doorknob; the door is open a little. All it will take is for me to pull.

A furry black head shoves its way through the opening. Onyx meows at us.

"You have a cat?" Ford asks.

"He kind of moved in a while ago. I call him Onyx."

"Hello, Onyx." Ford bends to pet, but the cat pulls back into the house.

"He's not real tame yet. We're working on it."

"Maybe he wants me to come in."

I grip the doorknob, take a deep breath and pull the door open.

"Let's go," I say. "But I warned you." I step into the house, my heart pounding. I'm conscious of the stuffy air, the scent of dust now mixed with that of the cat's litter box. I walk down the short hall toward the kitchen. "Sorry about the smell. Some of the vents are covered, so I don't get very good circulation. Maybe I should open a window. Or maybe a few windows." I hurry to the kitchen sink and open the window. "There, some fresh air. That's better. Here, I'll open the patio door too."

"Rylan, stop. It's fine. I told you, I don't mind the clutter."

I stop halfway across the dining room, surrounded by boxes that seemed so important to me before. Suddenly, I feel tears. I blink hard but can't stop them.

"I don't know what happened," I choke. "Mom kept the house so clean and neat."

Ford pulls me against his chest. "It's all right."

"No, it's not. It started as a protection. I thought if I had all this stuff around me, I could keep the spirits away. But they just find me anyway. Look at what happened with Darby. If that really is Elsa, I brought her in."

Ford runs his hand over my hair, down my back. "You've had to go through so much. First the ghost sightings, then your mom's murder. Moving into this house must have been hard. So many memories. It's no wonder you buried the place in things. It's actually a common reaction to grief."

I lift my head and search his blue eyes. "It is?"

"That's what happened with my great aunt. She lost her husband, so she filled the house to fill the void. I've seen it lots of times on the job. Hoarding is more common than you think."

I flinch at the 'h' word, although I know that's what I'm doing.

"Rylan, is that you?" Mom calls from her room. I grow stiff, but Ford doesn't hear her, he has no idea.

I'm not ready for that discussion yet. Letting him into the house is enough for today, so I don't answer Mom.

"Now, let's see if we can find Darby," Ford says.

I'd forgotten about the bear.

"He's so big. Can't be that hard to find him." Ford glances around the room.

"Who's with you?" Mom asks. "Do I hear a man?"

"I'll check down the hall," I say, pulling away. "Wait here."

I leave Ford in the kitchen and hurry to Mom. I slide into her room and shut the door behind me.

"Hey," I whisper awkwardly.

"Is there a man in the house?" she asks. "Why don't you bring him in so I can meet him?"

"You've already met him. It's Ford Pierce."

"Is Keaton with him?"

"No. He's here to see me." I feel my cheeks pink. "I really should get back to him."

Mom studies me a moment. "I see," she says, with a hint of a tease. "About time you two figured it out."

Even in death, Mom knows me too well.

"Okay, now let me go. I'll be back later."

"Why can't I see him? I haven't talked to Ford in a long time." She moves toward the door.

"No," I say too quickly. I can't imagine having my mother's ghost and Ford in the same room. How would I pull that off? I can't let anyone know she's here. Not yet. "We have to go anyway. Just stay here." My whisper is growing desperate.

"Ok, dear. That's fine." She's losing interest. What's left of her mind easily gets distracted, despite being more in tune lately.

"Thanks, Mom." I back out of the door and close it, leaning on the wood for a moment.

"Were you talking to someone?" Ford asks from the end of hall.

How much did he hear?

"I was—I just—" I remember what we're doing here. "Darby is not in there."

I see him eyeing the stack of boxes in front of Keaton's door, a question in his eyes.

"Maybe we should look for Darby later," I say, leading him out of the hall. I don't want him anywhere near that room and what's locked inside.

When we return to the kitchen, I stop short. There on the dining table, leaning against a box, is Darby.

THIRTEEN

RYLAN FLYNN

"How the..." Ford says in awe. "He was not there a moment ago."

"That's what I've been saying. He just appears." I walk slowly toward the bear, prepared for it to move or lunge at me or something. He just smiles.

"Creepy thing, isn't it?" Ford says.

"I like him. Or at least I did."

"I did too. But now... wow."

We stare at the giant blue stuffed animal, neither of us wanting to touch him. "Now what?" Ford asks.

I think of the other haunted items I've destroyed—the black smoke that came out of them.

"I think we probably have to destroy the toy to release whatever is inside. I'll have to ask Lorraine to be sure. I hate to think little Elsa White is locked in there." I wave my hand in front of Darby's black plastic eyes. Ford is next to me and gently pokes it in the belly.

Darby's arm moves and I hear him say, "I love you."

I jump back and so does Ford.

"Did you hear that?" I ask in surprise.

"I didn't hear anything. You jumped and it made me jump. Did it talk again?"

"Now that I know, it does sound like a little girl. It really is Elsa. Poor thing."

I lean toward the bear. "Elsa, if you can hear me, we're going to get you out."

"Mommy?" My skin crawls with goosebumps.

"She wants her mommy. She sounds so scared."

"Maybe if we can bring it to her Mom, she can be released. Maybe that's why she's still here."

"That might work, if only Rochelle believed us."

"That's true. I don't think she'd even answer the door for us now," he says.

"We have to do something. Now that I know she's in there, I can't leave her alone. She's only seven."

"What do you have in mind?"

I reach for the bear and wrap my arms around it. "I'm bringing her with me."

Ford runs a hand over his short dark hair. "I guess for now that will work." He looks around the room and the piles. I can tell he wants to say something, probably about cleaning, but he doesn't.

I appreciate his silence on the topic.

Holding Darby, and Elsa, against my chest, I say, "Let's go work on the case. You're nice to help me with this, but I know you're itching to get after the killer."

His smile tells me all I need to know. "Let's go. I want to check out her apartment before we talk to Meera."

"How do you know Tyler's already been there?"

"It's the first place I would go if I was on the case. He probably went yesterday. They should be done checking it out by now. Hopefully, the coast is clear."

. . .

Kenzie lived in a top floor apartment, part of a large house that was divided into separate units at some point in the last few decades.

"That's her car." Ford points to a small hatchback parked in the street.

"So she must have been taken from here. Or someone picked her up."

"Let's go check out the apartment for signs of a struggle."

I leave Darby in the car, telling him to be good, and follow Ford across the yard.

A piece of yellow crime tape is strung across the entrance to a sketchy-looking set of stairs leading from the side yard to her door.

"Are we allowed to go up?" I ask, touching the yellow tape.

"Probably not, but we're going." Ford ducks under and starts up the narrow steps. I follow close behind, gripping the railing.

"I can't imagine moving furniture up these," I say as they sway a little under our feet.

"They've been here for years. I'm sure it's fine." He doesn't sound sure—he's put a hand against the siding as he climbs.

We reach the first landing. A door leads from here to the house. "Must be another apartment," Ford says. He stops and knocks on the door.

"What are you doing?" I ask, pressing tight to his back as a board creaks under my feet.

"Seeing if anyone is inside. I'm guessing no one lives here, or the tape would be after this door, not down the stairs. Too bad, they might have been a witness."

"Good point." We wait a few moments, but the door isn't answered. "Can we just keep going?" I ask as I look over the railing to the ground. We're only one floor up, but the ground seems far away.

I wonder how Kenzie felt about these steps. I hope she got a rent discount for having to use them. Maybe she wasn't afraid of heights.

We finally reach her door—a slab of metal, painted in faded red.

Ford tries the knob. "Locked," he says, reaching into his pocket.

"Now what?" I ask, holding tight to his arm.

He pulls out a small packet. "I came prepared." He opens the packet and takes out a lockpick set.

A few moments later, the door swings open.

The scent of cigarette smoke wafts out onto the tiny porch balcony. "Will we get in trouble for this?" I ask, peering into the dark apartment, but not walking in.

"Only if we get caught." He takes me by the hand and leads me inside.

I close the door behind us and give my eyes a moment to adjust to the dark apartment. All the curtains are closed. A sliver of light breaks through a gap—a shaft full of dancing dust cuts across the room to the faded floral rug.

The studio apartment is one big room, with two doors on one end. When Ford looks, the doors lead to a tiny bathroom and a tinier closet. There are dirty dishes in the kitchen sink and an open bag of bread on the counter.

The whole place smells like cigarettes, but I don't see any ashtrays.

"Did Kenzie smoke?" I ask.

"I don't think so, but it sure smells like she did."

"Maybe she quit when she started dating Eli. I don't think the Amish are big on cigarettes."

"That's for sure."

I cross to the unmade bed that fills most of the room. The blankets are a tossed mess—clothes are thrown in a pile at the foot. It reminds me of my own bed. I even see a stuffed bunny buried behind a pillow.

A stab of emotion, a mixture of anger and sorrow. I didn't know Kenzie, and her death hadn't really affected me. Until now.

My eyes sting and a sniffle catches me off guard.

"You okay?" Ford asks. His voice has a touch of a rasp to it.

"It just hit me. She wasn't much more than a girl. It's just awful that she was taken like she was."

Ford rubs my back. "I know."

We stand together, me staring at the messy bed, his eyes darting all around the room. I finally wipe my traitorous eyes and go back to studying the room, desperate to find a clue.

"Hard to tell if there was a struggle here," Ford says, all detective now. "The place is kind of a mess."

In one corner, things are piled up high. Not like my house, but it's obvious she had more stuff than would fit in this tiny apartment. Next to the pile, a dresser is overflowing, drawers open, but not tossed.

"Look at this," Ford says, pointing to a rack of shoes near the door. "Each space is full."

"Okay?" I ask.

"I don't see any other shoes lying around. Most likely this is all she owns."

"And she didn't have shoes on when I found her." I follow his train of thought.

"Or socks. I think she was taken from here. Was probably just home and barefoot."

"Makes sense," I agree. "So, who took her? There's no obvious signs of struggle. Nothing looks like it was stolen."

"It must be someone who knew her."

"And dragged her down those rickety stairs?" I asked.

"Maybe he made her walk? He could have had a weapon."

"But she wasn't shot or stabbed."

"Not that we know of. Neither of us got a good look at her. There could have been wounds we didn't see."

"We need to talk to Marrero and get his report," I say.

"Fat chance of that."

"Maybe Tyler will tell us. Or maybe it will be on the news. Cause of death is pretty basic information."

"I watched the news last night and this morning. They only said her body was found," Ford says.

"It's frustrating, isn't it?" I ask, with a touch of humor.

"What?"

"Trying to work a case when the police won't help you."

He looks abashed. "It is, but I stand by all the times I told you to stay out of it. This is different. This is family," he says sternly.

"Mickey is family."

"And that case almost got you killed, Rylan."

I don't want to get into it again. "Now we have each other to look out for the other. We'll be fine." A niggle of doubt moves through my mind. Whoever killed Kenzie had a reason. Coming here to get her wasn't a random act. This could be dangerous if we get too close.

"Are you sensing anything? If there's a ghost, that could really help us."

I'm surprised I hadn't already thought of that. I do a mental check of my body and surroundings.

"No. Sorry."

"Even in this old house?" he asks, hopeful.

"Not all houses are haunted."

"I know. But a witness that saw who took her would clear this case up pretty easily."

"It's never that easy."

FOURTEEN

RYLAN FLYNN

We leave the apartment and descend the shaking stairs. As I turn at the second-floor landing and look down the steps, I step back in surprise.

At the bottom, looking up, sits Darby.

I freeze on the landing. "She's getting more active," I say. "Now she's following us around."

The bear tips over.

"How did it get out of the car?" Ford asks, standing close behind me.

A quick glance at the Malibu and I see all the doors are still shut.

"Creepy," I whisper.

"Guess Elsa wants out now that we know she's there."

"If it is Elsa," I say under my breath.

"What else could it be?" Ford starts down the steps, making them sway.

I think of Keaton's room again. Did the thing inside get out? Is it somehow in Darby? That can't be. The voice is a little girl.

"You're right," I say, following him down. Once again on the ground, Ford picks Darby up and tucks him under an arm.

"I love you, Mommy," the bear says.

I brace for some reaction from Ford, but he just carries it to the car, oblivious.

"Sorry you got scared, Elsa," I say once settled in the car, the bear in the backseat.

"Do you think that's what she was doing? Looking for you?" Ford asks.

"Makes some sort of sense. She's been through a lot, with the cancer and passing and being locked in the bear. If she knows I'm here, she might be looking for comfort."

"Or her real mom. If only we can convince Rochelle."

"We could try her husband. We need to do something, and soon. I can't carry a huge stuffed animal with me everywhere. Plus, she needs to cross over. I wonder what she's waiting for."

"Probably to see her parents again. Let them know she's okay," Ford says reasonably.

"Is she okay, though? How do I explain this to them?"

The bear falls forward, presses against the back of my seat.

"Whatever we do, we need to do it soon. She's freaking out in there," I say.

"There has to be a way to get her out. Then she can cross," he offers.

"That might work. We could film it and see what happens. I'll ask Lorraine."

"Yes, yes, yes, yes," the bear starts chanting.

I turn around in my seat. Darby is rocking back and forth. "She's saying yes." I have to smile at Elsa's excitement. "She's ready."

"Let's do it tonight. Get Elsa off our plate so we can focus on Kenzie."

"I'm sorry," I say contritely. "I didn't expect to be dealing with a haunted toy during our investigation."

"Don't be sorry. At least we can help Elsa. All we can do is bring justice for Kenzie. It's too late to help her." We drive in heavy silence for several moments. "You didn't see her, right? There's no way her spirit is still here?"

"I didn't see or sense her. That doesn't mean she isn't here, just means I don't know. I really wish I could talk to her."

He squeezes the steering wheel hard. "I know. It's just—you should have seen my family yesterday. They are all shell-shocked. Owen told stories about her as a child. How she loved the piano since she was little. Took to it easily. How she loved animals, especially horses. This one time, she tried to cut her own hair and took a big chunk out of the back. Julia had to take her to the beauty shop and have it cut short." He smiles ruefully. "She was a really good kid. I wish you could have known her."

"She sounds wonderful."

Another long silence full of sadness. "What was the apartment number again?" Ford asks as we pull into the parking lot of a complex popular with the college-age kids.

"Seven-four-twelve-B," I say.

We park in front of the building marked 7412.

"Here we are." Ford looks through the windshield at the apartments. "Meera Sharma's. Owen also said Meera is Kenzie's best friend here in Ashby."

"Wonder if she knows about Eli?"

"One way to find out." He looks into the backseat. "What are we going to do with Elsa? Lock the doors?"

"The doors don't hold her anymore." I talk to the bear. "We'll be right back. I need you to be a good girl and stay in the car, okay?"

Darby doesn't move.

"I mean it. You can't get out of the car and scare people. Do you understand?"

Still no reaction. I decide to take that as a good sign and get out of the car. Even though it won't help, Ford locks the doors as we walk away.

We knock on Meera Sharma's door and wait. Music blares behind the door. A female voice sings along to "Loser" by Beck.

"Old school," I say about the music.

Ford knocks again, louder this time. "Meera? Can we talk?" he shouts.

The music suddenly stops. "Who's there?"

"I'm Detective Pierce," Ford starts. "We want to talk to you about Kenzie Odell."

The door opens slowly. A young Indian woman with eyes pink from crying peers out.

"I already talked to the detectives earlier. Do the police have more questions?" She leans against the door, not inviting us in, but not exactly blocking us either.

"I'm a detective, but I'm technically not on this case. Kenzie was my cousin, I'm looking into her murder. This is my friend Rylan," he adds.

I give a half smile to the distraught young woman. "Kenzie was my best friend." She sounds like she's about to choke.

"We know. Her dad told us," Ford says gently.

"Owen? He's a good guy. A bit overprotective, really. But not bad for a dad." Meera backs up and lets us into the apartment.

This apartment is much cleaner than Kenzie's, and a lot less cluttered. It's almost Spartan, there's so few things in the tiny living room. A small succulent plant on a table by the window is the only hint of decorating.

"Please sit," Meera says, waving toward a stiff gray couch. Ford and I perch on the cushions. "Can I get you anything? I have water, and—" She looks toward the spotless kitchen, then breaks into tears. "I'm sorry," she says, wiping her eyes on the hem of her T-shirt. "This has been so hard."

"I imagine," I say, remembering how I felt when Mickey was missing. I can't imagine what I'd do if she were gone. "We are so sorry."

"You know what I'm going through," she says to Ford. "She was your cousin. I remember her mentioning she had a family member that was police. It must have been you. We used to joke that she could speed because she could get out of a ticket."

"Sounds like her," Ford says. "Always joking around. How long have you two been friends?"

Meera pulls a straight-back chair from the tiny dinette into the living room, then sits between us and the TV. "We met in high school when she moved in with her dad. Guess her mom couldn't handle her or something. Kenzie was sweet, but a bit of a wild child. Her parents thought she would tame down in a small town like Ashby. Fort Wayne may not be the most happening city, but it's better than here for action."

"What kind of action are we talking about?" Ford asks.

Meera's eyes are guarded. "You know, kid stuff."

"I don't know. Why don't you tell us?" he says. "Just so we're all on the same page."

"Parties, hanging out. Things high schoolers do."

"Did you and Kenzie party a lot?"

Her eyes dart from his face to mine. "What's a lot? We had some fun. Who doesn't at that age? Of course, you being a cop, maybe you didn't."

"I had my share of fun. But I want to hear about Kenzie."

Meera stares openly at me. "Why do you look so familiar?" she asks. "Wait, I got it. You're the ghost hunter! I've seen all your episodes. Wow, your last episode. That was a tear-jerker for sure. Wow, *the* Rylan Flynn, in my apartment."

"Our last episode has been very popular," I explain to Ford.

"Something like a million views, right?" Meera asks.

She suddenly remembers why we're here and turns serious. "You didn't see Kenzie's ghost, did you? That would be so cool."

"I didn't. I'm sorry."

"Oh well. I guess you guys will still find out who did this to her, right?"

"We're doing all we can."

"That's what those detectives said. The lady one was so nice."

"Faith Hudson?" Ford asks. "She was here?" A tiny edge of envy creeps into his voice.

"Yes, her and that handsome one—Spencer, I think. They both asked me questions last night. They wanted me to come back in today for a follow-up, but I don't know what else I could tell them."

"Then why don't you tell us what you said," Ford prompts.

"All I know is Kenzie was great. No one would want to hurt her. Sure, she liked to party back in the day, but lately she was different. Much more stable. I know she was in love, but she wouldn't say with who. A friend can tell, you know."

"She didn't mention she was dating anyone?" Ford asks.

"Whoever it was, she kept it hush-hush. I got the feeling she thought I wouldn't approve. Maybe he was in jail or something. Like I would care. As long as she was happy, that's all I worried about."

"Does the name Eli Graber sound familiar?" Ford asks.

Meera thinks for a long moment. "There's that furniture company called Graber. Amish, isn't it? My parents bought a dining table from them. Good stuff, solid wood." Meera suddenly stops, then continues. "Wait, she was dating an Amish man?"

"Yes," I say. "For several weeks."

Meera shifts in her chair, crosses one leg over the other. "That explains a lot," she says absently.

"Explains what?" I press.

"Why she changed. She stopped hanging out with us. Even stopped drinking." She uncrosses her legs and leans forward. "I have to be honest with you, I haven't really seen her in a few weeks. She stopped returning my texts and calls. It was like she thought she was better than us."

"Who's us?"

Meera's dark skin pales suddenly and she looks away. "I don't mean us, I mean me. She stopped talking to me."

Ford and I exchange looks, not believing her. "Is there anything else you can think of? Anyone that would want to hurt her? Someone she was fighting with? Or owed money? Maybe a drug deal gone bad?" Ford asks.

"Kenzie wasn't into drugs. Not anymore. And I told you, she really changed the last few weeks. She wasn't ever into that kind of thing anyway." Meera stands and walks toward the door. "I'm sure you can understand all this has been very upsetting. I'd like to listen to music and grieve alone if you don't mind." She opens the door and waits for us to exit.

With no other choice, Ford and I leave.

Ford hands her his card. "You can call me, too, if you think of anything."

"Detective Pierce?" she asks as we start down the sidewalk.

Ford turns. "Yes?"

"Why did you get kicked off the case?"

"Because I care about Kenzie. We're not supposed to work on cases where the victim is too close."

She puts one hand on her hip. "But you're doing it anyway?"

"For her."

"I understand." She looks at the sidewalk for a long moment. She seems to make a decision. "Look, I wanted to—" She suddenly stops, her eyes looking behind us.

A young man walks toward us, a mop of curls hanging over his forehead. "Good afternoon," the young man says in a heavy British accent. He passes us as he greets Meera.

We wait for her to finish her thought, but she just enters the apartment with the British man and closes the door.

"Guess she's done talking to us," I say.

FIFTEEN

TYLER SPENCER

Faith Hudson holds the door to the coroner's office and lets a woman I recognize as a crime-scene tech exit. The tech smiles as she passes.

"Here to see Marrero?" the woman asks me.

"Yes. We're here for the autopsy report," I tell her. "How is he today?"

The tech gives a wry smile, says "good luck," and leaves.

"Is he really that bad?" Faith asks as we enter the building.

"Usually," I say. "He's not known for his friendly personality."

"I haven't met him yet, but I've heard things."

"If it was about his temper, then the stories are most likely true."

Faith pushes one of her long thin braids over her shoulder nervously.

"You've been through this before?" I ask.

"Lots of them back in Indianapolis, unfortunately. They are interesting."

"That's one way to put it. I've been to many of them, but it never gets easier." As we walk down the hall, I get the courage up to ask what's been on my mind. "If you were a detective back in Indy, why did you come here to Ashby and go back on patrol?"

"I figured you already knew," she hedges.

"I heard you moved back to town after a divorce, but I don't know more than that."

"Divorced, yes. And broke. He took everything. I had to move back here with my daughter, Halle. We're staying with my grandma. We had nowhere else to go."

"And there are no detective spots open here in Ashby."

She smiles with a touch of teasing in her expression. "Not yet. Just wait, I may be after your job."

I know she's just playing, but there's a note of truth. Faith has much more experience, and she might actually be after a detective spot. In our tiny department, that would mean replacing either Ford or me. Ford has more seniority. My job could be in danger.

Faith walks ahead down the hall, her long braids swaying behind her. She seems friendly enough, but I need to keep an eye on her.

We reach the door to Marrero's lab.

"You coming?" she asks, her hand on the knob.

I take a deep breath before knocking.

"Come," barks Marrero.

I push the heavy metal door—the scent of chemicals and death reach my nose. I make a conscious effort not to react. On the table lies the body of Mackenzie Odell, a white sheet draped over her.

"You're late," Marrero comments. I look at the clock. It's two minutes past the hour.

"We're here now." I try to keep my voice friendly. "What did you find?"

Faith is close to the body, studying Mackenzie's face. "So

pretty," she whispers. This is the first time she's seen her, since she was assigned to the case after the body had already been removed from the scene.

Marrero turns on a recorder, then snaps on his gloves. He gives the date, then starts in. "Present in this report are Detectives Tyler Spencer and..." He pauses, looking to Faith in question.

"Faith Hudson," she supplies.

"Right. The subject is Mackenzie Odell, twenty-year-old female. I suppose you want cause of death first?"

"Sure," I say.

"There's actually two, and it's impossible to say which killed her. See these marks here on her neck? She was strangled. Judging by the shape and placement of the marks, it shows it was manual. The hyoid bone in her throat is crushed as well, a clear indication of strangulation."

"And the second?" Faith asks.

Marrero lifts his head and stares daggers at her. "I was getting to that. The subject was also drowned. There's water in her lungs."

"So she was thrown into the water still breathing," I say.

"Or she was strangled while in the water. The amount of water was somewhat small for a drowning, but not impossible. That's why I said two causes. Either would have killed her, but my conclusion is that both combined were the ultimate cause of her death."

"Sexual assault?" Faith asks.

"No signs of assault, but she did have DNA inside her."

My ears perk up at this. "We have DNA?"

"Yes, there was biological evidence in her," he says flatly.

"Did you run it on CODIS? Was there a hit?" I ask.

"I ran it, but there was no hit. You'll have to find the possible contributor and make the comparison," Marrero says flatly.

"I know just where to start. We weren't able to talk to him

yesterday, but we'll find him today," I say, anxious to find Kenzie's boyfriend, Eli Graber. His family flat-out denied their relationship yesterday and wouldn't tell us where he was. Today will be different. I'm anxious to get going, but I know Marrero has more to tell us.

"As we saw at the scene, she has a cut on her hip." He pulls up the sheet to show us the area. "It is a precise cut, not from a branch or a rock or anything in the river. It's from a razor blade or a very sharp knife."

I look at the tiny patch of missing skin. "Why would the killer cut a piece of her off?"

Faith looks too. "Strange, a tiny perfect rectangle."

Marrero continues with the report, noting bruises on her wrists and scratches on the bottoms of her feet. "So her hands were tied and she was walked barefoot to the river?" Faith asks.

"Looks that way," Marrero concedes.

"That means the river was chosen as the murder site. She wasn't thrown over the bridge and floated to those branches," I say. "That place is so remote, it's a wonder she was found at all. Good thing Rylan happened by."

Marrero stiffens and I realize my mistake. "It's *your* job to find murder victims, Spencer. We don't need the help of that charlatan."

I want to defend Rylan, but I bite my tongue. It won't change his mind.

Faith looks from me to Marrero with keen interest.

"Thank you for the report," I say, ready to go find Eli and obtain a DNA sample.

"Just doing my job. Now go do yours." He turns off the recorder, then hands me the written report. There will be a digital version sent too, but he likes things done the old-fashioned way.

"Thank you," Faith says at the door. "It was nice to meet you in person."

"Enjoy playing detective," he responds. Faith flinches, opening her mouth to respond.

"Let's go." I open the door and usher her into the hall before she can. "Ready for a ride in the country?"

SIXTEEN

RYLAN FLYNN

Ford and I spend the rest of the afternoon tracking down Kenzie's few friends, from the list her dad made. Either no one else was home or they weren't coming to the door. I'm not sure how much it matters. From what we've seen so far, Kenzie liked to keep to herself. By late afternoon, I'm tired of knocking on doors and having nothing to show for it. It's also way past lunch time.

"You hungry?" I ask Ford as we sit at a red light.

"I could eat," he says. "What you have in mind?"

"We're close to The Hole. We could visit Aunt Val."

"You just want a donut." He smiles as the light turns green.

"That's just a bonus. I want to ask Val what she knows about Kenzie, if anything. You'd be surprised how much she knows about this town."

"I'm not surprised. Everyone around here finds their way to The Hole at some point."

Ford makes a right turn—we pass the courthouse. We get lucky and find a parking spot near the donut shop. I leave Darby in the backseat and tell Elsa to be good.

The smell of donuts fills the air and makes my stomach

growl. Aunt Val is wiping a table when we enter. She's alone in the shop.

She does a double take when she sees me with Ford. "Hey, Ry, Ford. Good to see you." She eyes Ford suspiciously. Their relationship has been strained ever since he wrongly arrested her for murder.

She shoots me a questioning look. I squirm under the scrutiny. Maybe this wasn't such a good idea, since I haven't told Val about the change in our relationship yet. I guess the cat's out of the bag now, so I take Ford's hand and say hi. Val meets my eyes, and I know she's dying to say something, but she has the good grace to take it in her stride.

"You two hungry?" she asks, tossing the towel on her shoulder. "We have these new sandwiches. Ham and cheese bagels." She goes back behind the counter.

I look to Ford in question, and he nods.

"Sounds great," I say. "Probably better for me than a donut."

"I'll take one too, please," Ford says, releasing my hand and reaching for his wallet. "To go."

Val starts making our sandwiches, then asks, "So, what are you two up to? Ford, I figured you'd be busy working the Mackenzie Odell case." Do I hear a tiny note of admonishment? "I saw it on the news. That's really something, isn't it?"

"Mackenzie is my cousin, so they took me off the case," Ford says.

"Oh no, I'm so sorry."

"Rylan and I are still working on solving it, though."

"Good for you," Val says to me as she hands over the sandwiches.

Ford pulls out his card, but Val refuses payment. "Your money is no good here," she says a bit stiffly, trying to be nice for my sake. "Now, is there anything I can do to help you catch this guy?"

"Did you know Kenzie? Did she come in here much?" I ask.

"I thought about it last night when I saw her picture on the news. I do remember her. She used to hang out with a group of kids around the same age. I remember them because they always wore dark clothes and heavy makeup. Sometimes, they'd come in when they should have been in school. I got the feeling they were troublemakers, although they never did anything wrong. Maybe talked too loud sometimes."

"You said school, like high school?" I ask.

Val nods.

"What about more recently? Did she still hang out with that group?" Ford asks.

"Now that you mention it, I don't think I've seen them all together for a while. She would come in with another girl. She was Indian, I think."

"That would be Meera," I say.

"She came in with that girl, but not with the guys."

"Guys?" Ford asks.

"The original group of them was the two girls and three guys. There's that British boy, Paul, and I think the other's name was Caleb. The third boy died a few years ago. His name was Miles."

I recognize the names—some of the friends that didn't answer their doors.

"Died how?" I search my own memory, looking to Ford for input.

Val shakes her head. "I might be wrong, but I think it was suicide. I don't remember the details."

"Do you remember?" I ask Ford. "Would you have been a detective then?"

"I don't think so, but I've seen a lot of that type of thing. When was this?"

Val scrunches her face, thinking. "Two years, maybe three?"

"Must have been while I was in narcotics."

"We can ask Owen. I'm sure he remembers," I offer.

"I'll ask him, but not today. They're at the funeral home making arrangements."

A silence falls over the shop. The door suddenly opens and two men enter, breaking the sad moment.

"Thanks for the help," I tell Val and step away from the counter. Ford heads for the door.

"Call me later," Val says, wiggling her eyes in a question at Ford's turned back.

"I will," I promise, following Ford outside to the car.

We settle into our seats and open our sandwiches. I take a big bite of mine and it's delicious. "I'll have to tell Val that these new sandwiches are a hit," I say once I swallow.

Ford is chewing, lost in thought. "I hate this," he says after a moment.

My stomach lurches. "Hate what?" I ask. Does he mean eating together?

"Being out of the loop. I don't even know her official cause of death."

"You could ask Tyler," I venture.

"That would just get him in trouble for helping me."

"Maybe if you talk to the chief, he'll put you back on."

"That's not going to happen. He was pretty adamant. I'm surprised I haven't been called into his office already."

"So, what do you want to do?"

He takes a bite of sandwich and continues thinking another long moment. "The computer will have the autopsy report," he suddenly says.

"So you just need to log in. Can you do that from home?"

"No. The system is protected. I can only log in from the office." He's growing excited. He wraps up the remainder of his sandwich and puts the car in drive.

"Where are we going?"

"I'm taking you home, and then I'm going to work."

I don't like the idea of being left out, but I understand. "Can you take me to Mickey's instead? My car is still there. Plus, I need to fill her in on what we've found."

When we get to Mickey's, my Caddy is in the street. Ford parks behind it but leaves the engine running.

"I guess I'll call you tonight." He looks in the rearview at the bear. "We need to release Elsa."

"I'll call Lorraine, and I want to talk to Mickey about it first, but yes, tonight."

"Your house?"

I stiffen. "You know I can't do that. Mickey doesn't know about all the stuff."

"She's never seen it?"

"Never. I always come here."

"Talk to her about Elsa and let me know." He's obviously anxious to get to the precinct. He even puts the car in drive before I get out. He does take the time to meet my eyes. "Thank you for your help. Seriously, I'm so glad you're here."

"Good luck with the computer." I stall, wondering if he'll kiss me goodbye, wondering if that's even appropriate right now.

He makes no move toward me. I push down the regret, and disgust at myself for thinking such thoughts.

"You know I want to kiss you goodbye," he then says with a little twinkle in his eye.

"Why don't you?" I didn't mean to say that out loud.

"Mickey's watching out the window and I don't know if you want her to see."

"I no longer care who sees," I say and lean in. His lips brush mine for the slightest of moments, leaving a trail of heat behind them.

"I'll call," he says.

"Let me get Darby," I say, climbing out, but not wanting to leave him. I open the back door and pull the bear against my chest.

"Bye, Rylan," he says as I shut the doors. I watch him drive away and squeeze Darby harder.

"Mommy?" Elsa says.

"Hold on, Elsa. I'll get you to your mother soon."

I turn toward the house and Mickey is coming out onto the front walk. "Spill it," she demands in a friendly way.

"I don't know what you mean," I play dumb.

"You leave me on the bridge in the middle of the night. You barely answer my texts for two days. Now I see you kissing Ford."

I shrug and feel my cheeks burning. "Things have changed."

"I can see that. I'm so glad you finally got the courage to admit how you feel."

I shift Darby onto my hip. "I just can't believe he feels the same way."

"Oh, Rylan. Everyone knew you two were going to end up together. It's just amazing how long it took you guys to realize it." She smiles and I can't help smiling back. "I want to hear all about it, but first—what's with the bear?"

SEVENTEEN

RYLAN FLYNN

I carry Darby as I would a toddler, propped on my hip, my arm around his waist. "This is Darby. Sort of," I tell Mickey as we go into her house. I put the bear down on the tan leather couch. Darby's bright blue fur seems out of place in the well-decorated room.

Mickey pats him on the head playfully. "He's cute."

"He's also haunted."

She snatches her hand back and gives me a look. "Haunted? Only you, Rylan."

"I bought him at a garage sale awhile back. At first, everything was fine. Then he started moving his arms."

Mickey eyes the bear from across the room. "Moving?"

"When he started showing up in different rooms, I knew he had a problem."

Mickey's eyes grow wide.

"Now he talks too."

Mickey approaches the couch to study him, leaning in, but not getting too close.

A stuffed arm shifts slightly and Mickey jumps.

"What the—"

"See? Haunted. We went back to the place I bought him and talked to the mom. She said her daughter, Elsa, died not long ago from cancer. We're pretty sure Elsa is in Darby."

"Does 'we' mean you and Ford?" she asks with interest.

"Um, yeah. We've spent the last two days together."

Mickey's eyebrows fly up. "All of the last two days?"

"Not like that. We didn't spend the night together."

Mickey seems disappointed. "I suppose you've waited this long. Plus, with a haunted bear and a murder, you've been a bit busy. I know Ford is off the case, but you two can't stay away from this if you tried. What have you found out?" Mickey sits in a chair as far from Darby as possible.

I sit on the couch, sinking deep into the cushions. "We haven't found much that's useful. Kenzie used to live in Fort Wayne with her mom, but she was running wild there, so she moved to Ashby to be with her dad. She was a bit of a wild child at high school here too, ran with a few other kids. She went to the community college but had to drop out. She did okay after that, had a tiny apartment all her own. Lately, she'd changed. Calmed down, dressed more plain, that sort of thing."

"Why the change?"

"Get this—she was dating an Amish guy."

"Amish? How did that happen?" Mickey asks.

"They met at that grocery in Wolcottville, and it just progressed from there."

"So the boyfriend killed her? Aren't the Amish generally against violence?"

"We don't have proof either way. Eli seemed crushed when he found out what happened."

"He could have been lying. Did he have an alibi?"

"I didn't ask." I spin my charm bracelet, concerned. "Why didn't I ask?"

Mickey shrugs. "Maybe you could talk to him again."

"I was lucky to talk to him the first time. We only knew where to find him because a ghost at the farm told us."

Mickey smiles knowingly.

"What?" I ask.

"I like you saying 'we' and 'us'. It's nice. I wondered if you two would ever figure it out."

"Why do you keep saying that?" I try for innocence. "I mean, maybe you knew I liked him, but he didn't like me back until just recently."

"Keep telling yourself that. It was obvious to me. But I've known you both forever. It's pretty romantic, don't you think?"

I look at the rug, unable to meet her eyes. "I guess."

"You'll get used to it. Just enjoy the ride." Mickey smiles smugly.

"We have to solve this murder first."

"Where is Ford now?" She leans back in her chair.

"He went to the precinct to look up the autopsy report. We don't even have a confirmed cause of death yet."

"I bet he's going nuts being left out," she says.

"A little. He feels responsible for his family to get justice for Kenzie." I tip my head back and let out a long breath. This moment of rest feels good.

"So, who are your suspects? Let's figure this out," Mickey says after I sit back up.

"We don't really have one besides Eli, and I don't know how I feel about him."

"You said she got into trouble a bit, back in the day. Could there be something from her past life?"

"Nothing we've found yet. No one wants to talk to us and, without the police backing, all we can do is knock on her friends' doors. We did talk to her best friend, Meera. She didn't have much information. She didn't even know Kenzie was dating Eli. It looks like Kenzie pretty much kept to herself lately."

"Don't you think that's strange?" Mickey asks, running her hand along the arm of her chair.

"What do you mean?"

"A girl her age not going out, not even telling her friend about a new man. What was she hiding?"

"I never really went out, and neither did you," I point out.

"I was married by Kenzie's age, so no, I didn't. You—well, you're unique."

I twist my bracelet again. "That's one way to put it. I was hiding from all the ghosts in this town. It was safer to just stay home."

"Right. Unique."

"Maybe Kenzie had a reason for not going out. Maybe she'd had enough of partying when she was younger. Got it all out of her system?" I try.

"Could be. I'm just looking at it from all angles. By the way, I did some digging. You know I love looking things up. I checked out her Instagram posts."

I grow excited. "What did you find out?"

"Not much, really. As you said, she didn't go out a lot. There were some posts from last summer, though. A lake party." Mickey pulls the pictures up on her phone, then hands it to me.

Kenzie and Meera are standing on the deck of a pontoon, both dressed in bikini tops and shorts. They are leaning into each other, laughing and having a good time. It's sad thinking that, less than a year after this picture was taken, Kenzie would lose her life.

"At least she had some fun," I say, zooming into the picture to see Kenzie better. Anything to erase the image I have of her in the river.

And the crab in her mouth.

"She was so pretty," I say, my fingers still on the screen. The picture shifts and is now zoomed on Meera's shorts. Before I can zoom back out, I see something dark peeking out of her waistband.

I zoom in on the area until the shadow takes shape—170621.

"Look at this." I show it to Mickey.

"A tattoo. So? Even I have one."

"I know, but Eli said Kenzie had two. A butterfly on her shoulder and numbers on her hip. Meera has one in the same spot. Of the same thing."

"Again—so? We talked about getting matching ones, but you always chicken out."

"I know, but this one is just numbers. One-seven-zero-six-two-one."

Mickey looks at the picture. "That's a strange tattoo to get. What does it mean?"

"Eli didn't know. Kenzie said it was a drunken thing she did. He got the feeling she regretted it."

"I doubt it means anything. Nearly everyone has a tattoo these days." Mickey looks at her ankle and her own rose tattoo. "Maybe it's a birthday. Lots of people get those."

"Those numbers don't work as a date. There's no seventeenth month."

"Oh, yeah. Well, a serial number? Their favorite, uh, something."

"Could be. But favorite what?" I ask.

"Maybe we can ask Meera," Mickey offers.

"She did talk to us this morning. She might talk to me again."

Mickey stands up. "Let's go."

"Really? You want to come?"

"You can't have all the fun. And I found the picture."

I pull Darby into my arms.

"You're bringing the creepy bear?" Mickey asks.

"I don't want to leave Elsa alone. She gets scared and moves around."

Mickey gives an exaggerated shiver. "Like I said. Creepy."

"Are you free tonight? Around midnight?" I ask.

"Midnight? That sounds ominous. Why?"

"Ford and I want to do something to release Elsa. I'm going to ask the White Witch, Lorraine, to help."

"Release her how?" Mickey asks.

"Not sure yet. Destroy the bear in some way. I just don't want to hurt Elsa in the process."

Mickey stares at Darby. "I saw something on a movie once where they burned a possessed jewelry box." She shrugs. "Maybe something like that will work."

"Burn the bear? That might do it."

"Burn it at midnight? You sure have a flair for the dramatic." She gathers her purse and heads for the door.

"I'd like to film it too. Can you come?"

"How can I miss that?"

On the drive to Meera's, I call Lorraine. She seems surprised to hear from me, but when I explain about Darby, she grows interested.

"The bear is talking and moving?" Lorraine asks. "How interesting."

"I'm pretty sure it's the little girl who owned the bear inside it. She died recently from leukemia."

"A tragic death could cause a haunting," she says. "I've seen it before."

"Will burning release her?" I ask.

"Burning? Where did you get that idea?" she asks. I can hear her bracelets jangling.

"From a movie actually. I know it's a bit far-fetched, but would it work?"

There's a long pause as Lorraine thinks. "Let me look something up real quick." More jangling of bracelets—I can hear her muttering. "Yes, here it is. It says that burning should release the spirit inside. This is pretty advanced stuff. Maybe I should come help you."

"I'd really like the help. I'd appreciate it."

"Just tell me when and where. I'm quite interested now."

"We're doing it at midnight. I'll text you the address."

I end the call.

"Sounds like that went well," Mickey says.

"She's going to help tonight."

"That should make some good video. Lorraine is the only person I know who's more dramatic than you."

EIGHTEEN

RYLAN FLYNN

Mickey stands just behind my shoulder as I knock on Meera's door. This time I don't hear Meera singing, just the low murmur of a TV. She doesn't answer right away. I begin to wonder if she's really at home or just left the TV on.

Then I hear quiet talking behind the door.

"I don't know," Meera says, and suddenly opens the door. "Oh, it's you," she says. "I told you everything I know earlier. I have no idea what happened to Kenzie, or who hurt her."

"I just want to ask you another question," I say. "This is my friend, Mickey, by the way."

Meera's dark eyes flick to Mickey, then back to the floor and my Chuck Taylors.

"Who is it?" a distinctly British voice asks from inside the room.

"Just some lady that's working on Kenzie's case," Meera says to who I'm guessing is Paul.

He joins us at the door. "Are you with the police? We already talked with the detectives."

"I'm not directly with the police. More like a consultant," I explain.

"And you?" he asks Mickey.

"I'm here with her," she says, surprised to be singled out.

"We don't have anything more to say. You can go now." He reaches to close the door, but I shove my foot in the way.

"We just want to ask Meera a question about her tattoo," I say.

The young man flinches. "What about her tattoo? I don't see how that's any of your business."

I direct my attention to Meera, who's standing behind Paul. "Do you have a number tattooed on your hip?"

She raises her hands as if to ward us off but says, "No. I don't know what you're talking about."

"We saw it in a picture on Instagram," Mickey says, holding out her phone for Meera and Paul to see.

They look at the picture, then exchange a look. "Okay, maybe I do. So what?"

"We heard Kenzie has the same tattoo. The same number. What does it mean?"

They exchange another look that I don't understand. "It's just a random number," Meera tries, but it's obvious she's lying. "We'd been drinking and couldn't decide what to get, so we made it up." She self-consciously puts a hand over her hip.

"Is that all? Seems a strange thing to have tattooed on your body," I say.

"Like I said, we were drinking. We thought it was funny at the time," Meera says.

"Look, if you truly are helping the police to find Kenzie's killer, I'm sure you have better things to do than harass Meera about a bad decision," Paul says.

"We're just talking. Why don't you want her to talk to us?" I ask.

"Goodbye," he says and shuts the door before I can shove my foot back.

"Well, that happened," Mickey says as we stare at the closed door. Behind it, the TV turns up loud.

"We learned something, though," I say. "It wasn't a total loss."

"That drunk girls make bad choices?"

"That there's something to the number. Why else would she try so hard to hide it? Plus, did you see the looks they kept giving each other?"

"I more got the feeling that we were annoying them, not that they were hiding something."

My mind races with possibilities, but none of them make sense yet.

"Maybe we can ask her parents about the guy," Mickey says.

"We can't talk to Owen and Tammy, or even her mom right now. They're making funeral arrangements today."

"That sounds awful."

"It is." I think of picking out Mom's casket, all the tiny, unimportant decisions that have to be made. Keaton was with me, but he wasn't much help. He was so deep in grief he could barely talk, let alone decide on music for the funeral.

It all fell on my shoulders.

Later, when Mom reappeared in her room, I wondered if she knew about the funeral, what I had chosen for her.

I never asked.

Luckily, Darby is still where I left him in the backseat when we return to the car.

"What do you want to do now? Is there anyone else we need to talk to?" Mickey asks as she checks her phone.

"I don't know. I guess I wait for Ford to call. He went to the precinct to see the autopsy report."

"You won't believe this," she says in shock, reading something on her phone. "It's an email from WMEE. They want us to go on their morning show to interview us about *Beyond the Dead*."

"The radio station? How did they hear about us?"

"Remember when I told you we were getting amazing hits on the last episode? Well, double that in the last two days. We're almost famous, at least a little bit."

My mouth falls open and I gawk at her. "Seriously?"

She grins and nods. "Millions of views. Can you believe it?"

"Millions? Our little ghost hunter show?"

"Yep. Who would have thought?"

I drive in happy shock. This is what we've both been working for. "So, what does this mean?" I ask.

"Means we're going to be on the radio. Who knows where that may lead. We've gotten a bunch of requests for us to come check out suspected hauntings. I figured once you solve the Kenzie case, we'd get back to work."

"Just think of all the endorsements we could get," I say dreamily.

"I could pay off Marco's truck."

"I could, I don't know, get a car made in this century." I pat the dashboard of the old Cadillac.

"Look at us, dreaming big," Mickey says, obviously pleased.

"When does the radio want us?"

"They said as soon as possible. You know how it is—today we're hot, tomorrow we might not be. How about tomorrow? We could talk about the bear thing you want to do tonight."

"I need to talk to Elsa's parents again before I say that on the radio. Her mom was not receptive at all about ghosts. I hope once Elsa is freed, they'll come around. I'm guessing by all the times she's told me 'I love you' and called me mommy that she wants to talk to them. I'm not sure how to make that happen."

From the backseat, I hear, "I love you, Mommy," over and over.

"You don't hear that?" I ask Mickey.

"Hear what?"

"Elsa is talking. She won't stop." I glance into the rearview at the bear. "Okay, Elsa, I hear you. You can be quiet now."

"I don't know how you do it," Mickey says, suddenly serious.

"What do you mean?"

"Seeing all that you see, and hearing what you hear. It must be exhausting sometimes. You handle it all so well. I forget that it must be a burden occasionally."

"I love you, Mommy. I love you, Mommy. I love you, Mommy."

"Yeah, sometimes. Like now, when a little girl won't stop talking." I raise my voice and direct the last part of the sentence to the backseat.

Elsa abruptly stops and it's quiet in the car again.

"Thank you," I tell her.

The bear tips over in the seat.

Mickey spins at the sudden movement.

"Looks like she's not happy with being told what to do," she teases.

"Just a few more hours and she'll be out of the bear. We'll see how she feels then."

We've made it across town toward Mickey's house. "Are you taking me home?" she asks.

"I thought so. I don't know what else to do until I hear from Ford."

"Maybe we should go talk to the ghost at the bridge, Hazel. She might remember something helpful, now that the police have left and things have settled down."

NINETEEN

FORD PIERCE

I feel like a thief sneaking into the precinct. I don't really need to sneak. I do work here still. I've come in on my day off before. It's not that unusual.

Knowing I'm going against a direct order by Chief McKay makes me extra cautious. He won't be happy to see me.

I drive around the parking lot and don't see the chief's Suburban in its regular spot. Thinking I'm in the clear for the moment, I park near the back door and hurry across the lot. When I'm a few steps away, the glass door opens.

My heart jumps when the chief walks out. He stops short and stares at me.

"Pierce?"

"Hey, Chief." I try to look casual, like I belong here right now. "I didn't see your car."

"Drove the wife's. I thought you had the day off. Shouldn't you be with your family right now?"

"I, uh, I need something from my desk."

His eyebrows raise a fraction. "Something from your desk?" He doesn't believe me.

"Yeah. I left my..." I can't think of anything. My desk is

pretty empty, with almost no personal effects. I should've thought of a cover story before I tried coming here.

"You sure you're not here to check on the Odell case? I know the autopsy report came in today. Look, I can sympathize with what you're going through, how much you want to catch this guy, but you know as well as I do that having a family member on the investigation might mess up the case when it goes to court. We have to do this the right way."

"I won't mess the case up. I just need to get to my desk for a few minutes."

He's standing between me and the door—I step around him.

"Pierce, I'm serious."

"I know. So am I." Hoping I'm not trashing my career, I open the door and enter the precinct. I half expect the chief to follow me, but I don't look back.

I pass a patrolman on my way to my office. He nods but doesn't question me.

It's not until I reach the office door that I remember Tyler. What if he's inside at his desk? I can't snoop through the computer with him watching.

Taking a chance that he's out working the case, I push the door open.

The office light is on, but there's no one inside. I quickly shut the door behind me, then turn on the computer. My heart pounds as I wait for it to load. It's a strange blend of emotions to be in my familiar office and so nervous at the same time.

I rotate back and forth in my chair as the computer takes forever to come online. When it finally does, I log into our system and type in Kenzie's name.

I don't get any results and stare at the computer in confusion.

Then I realize I'd typed 'Kenzie' not 'Mackenzie'. I fix the error and wait again.

Finally, her report comes up. I don't take the time to read it now, I just send the whole file to the printer next to my desk.

I hear voices in the hall while I wait for the printer to start printing. "Hurry up, you stupid machine," I whisper, afraid it might be Tyler or, worse, the chief.

The printer starts spitting out pages that I collect as each appears. I glance toward the door as the last one comes out. Someone is in the hall, right outside the door. I tuck the pages under my shirt and sit at my desk. I grab a random file from the stack in the corner and open it.

As I pretend to read the report, the voice in the hall fades away.

I hurry to the door and crack it open. A quick glance both ways and the coast is clear.

Holding the file against my belly under my shirt, I walk directly out the back door. I don't see anyone, and soon I'm in my car.

I breathe a sigh of relief and take the pages from my shirt. I want to read them now, but I don't want to be seen. I drive out of the parking lot with no particular destination. A few blocks away is a Walgreens, so I pull into there and park in the corner.

I scan the report until I find the manner of death—homicide. No surprise there, but seeing it on official documentation makes my stomach sour. I skip to cause of death—asphyxiation or drowning. I read on about marks on her neck, water in her lungs, petechiae of the eyes a sign of asphyxiation.

As I read, the anger grows. This isn't some stranger the report is talking about. I picture someone's hands around Kenzie's throat as he holds her underwater. My own hands clamp into fists.

I force myself to finish reading the report. When I get to the part about a missing piece of skin on her hip, I remember what Eli said about a tattoo. Some number. Why would anyone want to cut a number off? What did the number mean?

I read the report from start to finish a second time, then sit it on the passenger seat and stare at a tree branch swaying against a bright blue sky.

The sky feels wrong, it doesn't match my emotions. It should be dark out, or at least cloudy. The information in the report weighs heavily on my heart. I almost wish I hadn't read it. I watch the tree branch for a long time, my mind swirling with where to go next, who to talk to, what to do. An ache of grief seeps into me—it's paralyzing.

For the first time since she was found, I let in the full impact of Kenzie's death. Quiet sobs tear my chest as I think of the pain my family is going through. She may only have come to us a few years ago, but she made an impression. She was loved, and those I love are hurting too.

I give into dark thoughts, thankful I parked facing the tree in the corner.

As I watch, the sun dips and the sky turns pink. I realize I've been sitting in this parking lot for way too long. I wipe my eyes with the back of my hand and take a deep, steadying breath.

My mind slides to Rylan, and I wonder what she's doing. I told her I would call when I got the report. I told her I'd help with Darby tonight. I told her I appreciate her help with the case.

I haven't told her the full extent of my feelings for her.

Those three words flit through my head, filling me with a mix of excitement and fear, but feeling right.

Everything with Rylan feels right—even tracking a murderer together.

I look at the empty passenger seat. She should be sitting there, with me. I take out my phone and call.

"Hey," I say when she answers, suddenly feeling shy at the sound of her voice.

"Want to go talk to a ghost?" she asks.

Despite my earlier grief attack, my heart lightens at the

thought of seeing her in action. Those three words play in my mind again, but I know now is not the time. "I'm in," I say instead. I pull out of the parking lot, thinking that I'd follow her anywhere.

TWENTY

RYLAN FLYNN

Mickey smiles smugly when I hang up the phone.

"What?" I ask, feigning innocence.

"You guys are cute. I like it."

"Stop," I say, but I can't help smiling as we drive out of town toward Ostermeyer Road.

We arrive at the bridge as the last rays of sun dwindle away. The encroaching darkness lends an otherworldly quality to the trestle bridge. The shadows of the metal beams fade as we pull over.

"Is she here?" Mickey asks.

I look through the windshield, searching for any sign of Hazel. My back isn't tingling, and I don't see her glow.

"Let's get out," I say.

The frogs are singing as the water whispers under the bridge. Our footsteps seem loud in the gathering evening.

"Hazel?" I call, then wait. "I'm not getting anything." I turn around in a slow circle.

"Wonder where she went?" Mickey says, camera in hand.

"She said she isn't always here. We must have missed her."

We look over the side to where Kenzie was found. I shine my phone flashlight. The bank is full of footprints.

"Looks like the techs were busy," Mickey says. "Think they found anything?"

"If they did it should be in the report Ford got from the precinct. Pretty sure he printed everything."

Mickey shakes her head. "What a place to die," she whispers and turns around, leaning her back against the railing.

"Can you imagine jumping from here and splashing in?" I ask, leaning over, shining the light on the water. "That must be a rush."

"You can have it. That's a long way down for me," Mickey says.

Tires crunch gravel on the side of the road as Ford parks behind my car.

A jolt of excitement shoots in my belly and a tingle climbs up my back. The combination of sensations swamps me.

I wave to Ford, surprised as usual at how handsome he is in the rising moonlight. He walks across the bridge to where we wait, Hazel trailing behind him.

"Why are you all here again?" Hazel asks as Ford says hello. He flicks a look over his shoulder as if he knows he's being followed.

"The ghost is behind you," I say.

"Really? I can sort of sense something behind me. Like when you can tell you're being watched."

Hazel leans into Ford's face, so close her nose almost touches his.

"Hazel, back up. That's not nice."

She focuses on me. "I'm just getting a good look. I can't hurt him." She leans in again, waving her hand in front of his face. "This one's your boyfriend, right?"

"Yes, now leave him alone."

"Sorry," she says with a touch of sarcasm. "Not like he can see me."

"What's she doing?" Ford asks.

"She was just in your face, but she's backed off now."

Mickey has the camera on, filming my half of the encounter.

"Do you mind if we ask you a few questions and film it like last time?" I ask.

Hazel turns her scrutiny to the camera. "What do you film? This camera can't see me, right?" She waves at the camera.

"No, but people like to watch me talk to ghosts like you."

"People are weird." She turns away from the camera. "Now, what do you want to know?"

"We're working on finding who killed Kenzie. We just wondered if you remember anything that might be helpful. Anything at all."

"I don't think I have any information for you. I told you, I wasn't here, and then she was down there when I got back."

"Back from where?"

Hazel just blinks. "Why? I thought this was about the dead girl."

"I'm just curious. Where do you go when you're not here? I've always wondered about that."

"I don't know." She sounds vague. "I don't know anything."

I tell the camera what she said.

"The smallest detail might help," Ford says. "You must know everything that's on the banks. Did the killer leave anything behind?"

Hazel looks over the side. "All of it is gone. All the trash."

I tell Ford what she said.

"The crime-scene techs took all the trash and bagged it as evidence. We don't know what might be useful, but you could."

"They always leave stuff, beer cans and cigarette butts. I wish they wouldn't."

"Who?" I ask.

"The teenagers that party here. They're the ones that left the trash. They come to jump in the water, and they stay and drink and things."

"Did you ever see Kenzie here?" I ask.

Hazel thinks for a few moments. "I think she used to come here, but I haven't seen her in a long time. Two winters since they came."

"Who was she with?" Ford asks after I repeat what she said.

"I don't remember. Friends I think." She suddenly looks me in the eye, then looks away. "I don't want to talk about it."

"Why not? Did something happen?" I press.

"I can't help you, and you can't make me talk. I told you, I don't know anything." Hazel backs away from us, pulling on the rope around her neck nervously.

"Please, Hazel. We just want to know what happened to Kenzie. What are you afraid to tell us?"

"I'm not afraid." She stops backing away and lifts her chin. "It just—it was horrible, and I can't believe it happened again. It's my fault. I should have been here. I could have saved him."

I quickly tell Ford what she said. "Saved who? What happened?" he asks.

"He did it to himself, just like I did." She rubs the rope marks on her neck.

"Tell us what happened," I prod gently.

"I was—uh, not here. When I came back, he was just hanging there." She points to the side of the bridge. "Just like I was. Just like I did. The exact same spot." Her voice cracks.

"When?" I ask.

"A few years ago. Two winters."

"What does this have to do with Kenzie?"

"He was her friend. I saw them here together, all of them."

I don't know what to make of this information. Val told us Kenzie lost a friend, but I didn't know he committed suicide at the same place she was murdered. It can't be a coincidence.

I tell all to Ford. Mickey keeps filming.

"Who else was she with?" Ford asks.

"I don't know. People. Teenagers that leave a mess."

I ask for Mickey to pull up the picture of Kenzie and Meera on a boat to show to Hazel.

"A picture in a box," she says about the phone. "How interesting."

"It is interesting, but do you recognize the girls?"

"That one is the dead girl."

"Right. How about the other one?"

"She's been here. She came with the boys."

"How many boys?"

"Three, including the one that hung himself here."

I tell Ford what she said.

"Do you know any names? Anything that will help us identify them?" he asks.

"No names, but one of them talked funny."

"Talked funny. Do you mean with an accent?"

Hazel refuses to tell us anything else. She grows more agitated and backs away down the bridge.

"Hazel, we need your help," I try.

She finally says, "I don't have to talk to you," and disappears.

Mickey turns off the camera. "Well, not sure that helped," she says.

"We found out that Kenzie's friend died here too. That can't be a coincidence, can it?" I ask.

"But what does Miles's death have to do with Kenzie's?" Ford asks.

"Maybe nothing," I say.

"But it could be something," Mickey says. "Maybe we should talk to Meera again, and her British friend."

"What about the third guy? Who is he?" Ford asks.

"Val said Caleb, or something similar. Meera will know

more," I say. "Tomorrow, we go back to her apartment. I don't know what else we can do tonight." I check the time. It's still a few hours until midnight. "What do we want to do before we release Elsa?"

"I need to get home. Marco will be wondering what I'm up to," Mickey says. "Where do you want to meet tonight to film the Elsa thing?"

I glance at Ford. My house is the most obvious place, but I don't want to do it there. Ford lives in an apartment, so that won't work. That leaves Mickey's.

"What about your backyard? You have the firepit on your patio. We could do it in that."

"I don't think Marco would like that."

"Maybe we need Dad's help on this one. I could ask about doing it in his backyard," I offer.

"Burn a haunted bear at a pastor's house?" Mickey asks.

"Why not? It's perfect. I'm not even sure burning the bear will release Elsa. We might need some prayers to help her."

TWENTY-ONE

TYLER SPENCER

The Graber Furniture Company sign sits at the end of a lane leading to an unassuming pole barn. Buggies are parked on one end of the gravel lot, cars on the other. Judging by the number of cars, the Amish furniture business is booming.

"Think he's here?" Faith asks. "Maybe we should have called first."

"Better to catch him unaware. If he's our killer, he'd definitely run if he knew we were coming."

"And they would cover for him, like they did at his farm."

"Precisely," I reply as I climb from the car. We drove my unmarked personal car instead of a cruiser to avoid drawing attention. Still, a man by the buggies looks on with interest. He has a beard, which signifies he's married, so I know it's not Eli. I raise a hand in greeting as we make our way toward the front door.

The man barely waves back, then looks away.

"Not the friendliest of people, are they?" Faith comments.

"They don't really like outsiders. Though they have to deal with them a lot."

"I haven't dealt with the Amish much. Not like this. We don't really have them around Indianapolis."

"I suppose not." I hold the door open for her. The scent of sawdust and wood wafts out. It reminds me of my grandpa's woodshop in his garage.

"Smells good in here," Faith says as we enter the showroom. All around us are handmade pieces of furniture, all of them solid wood. Even to my untrained eye, it's obviously quality. A dark-stained, heavy bedroom set catches my eye. I wish my paycheck would allow me to purchase something so nice. I'll have to settle for my mismatched set, but maybe someday.

"Hello. Welcome to Graber Furniture," an Amish woman in a dark maroon dress and white cap says. "Please, look around and let me know if you need anything." The woman is polite but looks at Faith with interest. As if she hasn't seen many Black people before.

For her part, Faith is trying not to stare at the Amish woman but is obviously curious.

"We're actually here to see one of your workers," I say. "Is Eli Graber here?"

The woman blinks in surprise. "Eli is in the shop. What do you want with him?"

"We're with the Ashby police. We need to talk to him. Can you lead us there?" Faith asks, stepping forward.

The woman pales. "Why do the police need to talk to Eli? He didn't do anything."

"Do you know Eli well?" I ask.

"He's my cousin."

"I assure you, he's not in trouble, but it's imperative we speak with him."

"Of course, of course." The woman leads us to a door at the far end of the showroom. The scent of wood grows stronger as we near it. The door is solid wood, six-paneled with a brass handle. The woman rests her hand on the handle, then turns to us.

"Maybe I should just go in and get him," she hedges. "I really shouldn't let you back here. It's off-limits to customers."

"We're not customers," Faith says. "Open the door."

She hesitates but eventually opens the door. "He'll be in the back, by the lathes."

The wood shop is expansive and full of activity. A man near the door looks up and speaks to the woman in fast Pennsylvania Dutch. I don't understand the words, but the tone clearly shows he's not happy she let us in.

She replies and I understand only one word, "Eli."

The man shouts something in Dutch across the room. A young man looks up suddenly, his eyes going wide when he sees Faith and me.

We hurry around the machines toward Eli. His eyes dart to the man that shouted, and he says a string of words in Dutch.

"Eli Graber?" I ask, approaching slowly.

"Yes," he says, straightening his back.

"Can we speak outside?"

"Whatever business you have with my son, you can say it here," the older man says. He's now standing beside Eli. "I'm Aaron Graber. Who might you be?"

"Detectives Spencer and Hudson with the Ashby police. We need to talk to Eli."

"About what?" Aaron asks defensively.

"About the murder of Mackenzie Odell."

"He doesn't know anyone by that name, do you, Eli?"

Eli looks at the sawdust-covered floor. "Actually, I do."

Aaron is shocked. "You know a murder victim? Eli, you better tell me what's going on."

I step in. "Eli was dating Mackenzie. She was found drowned and strangled under a bridge. DNA was found in her, and we need to get a sample from Eli to see if it matches."

Eli's skin is pale—he looks like he might be sick. "My DNA?"

"There's no way that anything belonging to Eli would be on a dead girl," another man joins the conversation. His long gray beard is impressive. He reaches a hand to shake mine, his eyes flicking over Faith. "Elisha Graber, Eli's grandfather, and owner of this store."

I shake the man's hand and introduce us again.

"We can get a court order for the sample, but we're hoping you'll give it voluntarily."

Eli's eyes dart from face to face.

"Go ahead," Elisha says sternly. "You have nothing to hide."

"I—I mean, my DNA could be on her." Eli hangs his head.

"What do you mean? You mean you and she?" Aaron asks, shocked.

Eli lifts his head, looking his father in the eye. "Yes. I loved her."

Aaron and Elisha begin yelling in Dutch and Eli shouts back. They argue for a few moments, then Faith interrupts.

"Look, you all can argue after we leave. We're here for the DNA sample and we won't go until we get it." The three men stare at her in surprise.

"Yes, ma'am," Eli says. "What do I need to do?"

Faith takes the swab kit from her bag. "I'm going to rub this on the inside of your cheek. It won't hurt." She holds the cotton swab up. "Now, open your mouth." She sounds like a mother— Eli obeys. "See, that wasn't so hard."

Aaron and Elisha look at Faith with new respect.

"How long until you know if the DNA is Eli's or not?" Elisha asks.

"We'll put a rush on it. Should have a result maybe tomorrow," I say.

"What if it matches?" Eli asks. "I already told you it might. I was with her the night before she was murdered."

"Can you prove it was the night before? Did anyone see you with her?"

"No. We just met at the park where we always meet. No one saw us."

"The park?" Elisha asks, then begins chastising Eli in Dutch again.

"Unless you can prove your encounter was the night before, and not the night she was murdered, I have to be honest, this doesn't look good for you." I can't imagine this fresh-faced young man with his hands around Kenzie's neck, but I can't rule it out either. "Do you have an alibi for the night she was murdered?"

He looks at the floor again. "I took the buggy out and just drove around."

"Did anyone see you? Did you talk to someone while you were out?" Faith asks.

"No. I was alone. I just wanted some air."

Kenzie's lifeless body on the table in Marrero's lab flashes through my mind. We could be talking to the man who put her there, no matter how innocent he looks.

"We'll be in touch when the results come in. If this DNA proves you were with her the night she was murdered, we'll be back with a warrant for your arrest," I say sternly.

"My arrest?" Eli squeaks. "But I didn't hurt her."

"Someone did, and right now you're our only suspect," Faith says.

Elisha steps between Eli and us. "I'm afraid you need to leave. You got what you came for. The test will prove Eli is innocent." He and Aaron cross their arms with Eli behind them. A wall of protection.

There isn't anything left to say, so we walk across the shop to the door. The other workers have all been watching—they cross their arms too. We can't reach the door fast enough.

"Well, we got the sample, but that didn't go too well," Faith says once we're back in the sunshine.

"Do you think he did it?" I ask.

"Odds are he did. I've seen it lots of times. Besides, it doesn't matter what I think. If this test comes back that he was with her, that cinches it."

"What about his story that he was with her the night before?" I ask, standing by the car.

"A likely story from a guilty man. He has motive, and we both know the boyfriend is always suspect one. Maybe she was tired of being a secret from his family and wanted to go public. That could ruin an Amish man, couldn't it?" Faith asks.

"I suppose it depends on the family. The Grabers are pretty big around here. I can't imagine Eli dating an English woman would go over well."

"Like I said, motive," Faith says.

"You're right, but we have to follow the facts." I climb into the car and shut the door. "Where to next?" I ask once seated.

Faith checks her phone for the time. "I need to pick up Halle from the sitter's soon. Do we have anything pressing that we need to do tonight?"

"I was going to go back to the office and run down a few things."

"You want me to help? I can do that work from home."

"No. It's already been a long day. You get your daughter, and we'll start again in the morning."

I leave Faith by her car in the precinct parking lot, then go to the office I share with Ford. I'm two steps into the room when I notice Ford's computer is on.

I'm sure it was off when I left.

TWENTY-TWO

RYLAN FLYNN

I don't want to ditch Mickey with my car again, so we drive back to town together. She checks her phone as I drive.

"I just got the email. We're confirmed to do *The Bill and Frank Show* the morning after tomorrow. Can you imagine us on the radio? That's bound to get more viewers to the show. This is so great."

Nerves assault me. "What will we say?"

"We just have to answer their questions, I guess. I've listened to the show lots of times. They'll probably ask you about the ghosts and make jokes like they always do. Do you think you're up for it? They asked for both of us, but you're the lead. You'll be the focus."

I think about this for a long moment. "Jokes? Do you think they'll make fun of me?"

"Bill and Frank make fun of everything. You can't take it personally. Come on. This could be so good for the show. You're kind of a big deal right now, even if you don't realize it. The views on the show are going sky high."

"I suppose if it helps the show, I can handle it. I've been made fun of before."

"They're fans, not enemies. They want us to come. Maybe they'll take it easy on us."

My nerves are still swimming, but I say, "I'm in."

I pull into Mickey's driveway as she grabs her purse from the floorboard. "I'll meet you at your dad's a little before midnight." She glances over her shoulder at Darby, still in the backseat. "You be good until then, Elsa."

The bear tips over on the seat, making us both jump.

"We definitely need to get her out of there," I say.

Mickey laughs anxiously. "Good luck."

When I get home, I see Ford's black Malibu is parked in front of the house. He's sitting on the chair by the front door, half-hidden by the shadows.

I take Darby from the backseat and approach. A tingle that has nothing to do with ghosts slides down my back. "Hey," I say, trying for casual.

"I hope it's okay I came by. I know your text said to meet at your dad's, but I wanted to see you." He stands and takes a step closer.

"Of course it's okay. You're always welcome here." My pulse quickens as he leans even closer. I sit Darby on the concrete walk.

Ford is just inches from my lips, hesitating. I press into him.

We kiss in the pale moonlight, my hands at the base of his neck. His hands find my hips, pulling me against him. My body molds into his, fitting perfectly.

He pulls his lips from mine and says, "We have some time to fill before midnight."

I lean my forehead against his collar bone. "What do you want to do?" I ask breathlessly.

"We could go inside," he says near my ear, his breath sending more shivers down my spine.

I press into him, reading his intentions clearly. I want to, I really want to.

Then I think of my room—of my bed. It's covered with clothes and stuffed animals. My room is hoarded even worse than the rest of the house.

I can't let him see.

I go still and he senses the change. "What's wrong? Am I moving too fast?"

"It's not that. I want to go inside. You have no idea how much I want to. It's just... The house—the stuff." I suddenly feel tears threatening. I rub my face against his shirt.

"I don't care about the stuff."

"I do. I just can't right now. I'm so sorry."

He rubs his hands down my back, soothing. "It's okay. Truly it is. Maybe tonight is not the night. I want it to be perfect for you. If you're not comfortable, then we will wait."

I didn't think it was possible, but I like him even more. "I'm so glad to have you," I whisper.

He leans back so he can see my face. "I'm glad for you too." My heart melts. I debate taking him in despite the state of my bedroom.

Then I hear the howl from inside and jump at the sudden sound.

Ford doesn't hear it, but the thing in Keaton's room screeches on and on. I want to cover my ears.

"What's wrong?" Ford asks.

Should I tell him about the thing in there?

"Nothing," I say, pulling away. My ears ache from the noise and I don't know how to explain what's happening.

Ford looks hurt. "Did I do something wrong?"

"No. It's nothing like that. It's a ghost thing. Let's just leave it at that." I can't take it anymore, I put my hands over my ears.

"You're scaring me. What's going on?"

The thing grows louder, the sound clawing the inside of my

skull. "I think you need to leave," I say miserably. "I swear, you didn't do anything. I'll explain someday, but I can't get into it now."

"Rylan, tell me."

I search his face. I know he'd understand.

I dive in.

"There's something locked in Keaton's old room. Something not of this world. It's mad that you're here and it's howling and screeching right now."

Ford takes a moment to let my words sink in.

"There's something in his room? I don't hear anything."

"You wouldn't. Only I can hear it."

"What is it? What's in there?" He takes a step toward the door.

"I don't want to get into it. For now, I just need you to go. I can't take this noise," I shout.

"Okay, okay. I'll go." He hesitates, putting his hand on my shoulder. "Will you be safe?"

"I've lived with it for years. I'll be fine."

Ford doesn't want to leave but finally says, "I'll meet you at your dad's." He kisses my cheek and hurries toward his car, looking back over his shoulder as he goes.

"Thank you," I call across the lawn, then I grab Darby and hold him against my chest, watching Ford drive away.

Once he's gone, the howling turns to laughter. I carry Darby to the back door and go inside. Once I'm in the house, the thing grows quiet.

I take Darby down the hall and stop by the stack of boxes blocking Keaton's door.

"I hate you!" I shout. I want to tear the boxes down, want to bust in and attack the thing.

But I know I won't win tonight.

"Rylan? Who are you screaming at?" Mom asks from her

room next door. For some reason, she can't hear the thing—she must never know it exists.

Everything crashes in, the thing, the stuff, Mom stuck on this side. I lean against the hall wall and slide to the floor. I pull Darby close and bury my face into his fur. I couldn't let Ford in. I don't know who killed Kenzie. Even the bear I hold is haunted.

It's all too much.

Tears burn and I can barely breathe as I sob into the stuffed toy. Thinking of Elsa inside, I cry even harder.

In my agony, I sense something beside me. I raise my head to see Mom sitting next to me. I've never seen her out of her room.

"How are you here in the hall?" I ask miserably, desperately wishing I could lean against her and feel her arms around me. A single touch from her could make this all better.

"You're crying," she explains. "I can't hear you in pain and not be by your side."

She reaches to push my hair off my face, but the hair doesn't move. Mom looks confused for a moment, then drops her hand into her lap. It breaks my heart even more.

"I love you, Mom," I say, leaning my head back against the wall, looking at the ceiling, sniffling.

We sit like this for several moments, just being together.

"This place is a mess," Mom says after a while. "Why are there so many boxes in the hall?"

"It's a long story." I stand and toss my hair over my shoulder. Stray strands stick to my wet face. I wipe them away with the hem of my T-shirt.

"That's a cute bear, though," Mom says.

"Thanks." I hold Darby on my hip. I debate telling her about Elsa, but instead, I lead her back to her room, afraid it'll take too much energy for her to be in the hall. "You should rest."

"So should you. You don't look too good. Did you eat dinner?"

I smile. Mom wanting to feed me makes everything feel normal.

"I'll grab something," I tell her. "Thank you for sitting with me."

"Anything for you, Rylan."

"I love you, Mom. I truly do."

"I love you too."

I watch her sit on the bed and pick up the brush. The hole in her head seems even more gruesome tonight.

Am I doing the right thing, keeping her here with me?

"Mom, are you happy here?"

She looks up in surprise. "Of course." There's a note of sadness. "I have you."

Is that enough?

Should I help her cross over? She doesn't even realize she's a ghost most days, but she's becoming more aware. Isn't that a type of life? How can I take that from her?

"Good night, Mom." I shut the door behind me, scoot past Keaton's room and stand in the doorway to my room. I find Onyx on my bed, sound asleep.

The room is a mess of boxes, clothes, stuffed animals, blankets and pillows. There isn't a bare spot on the floor. The chair in the corner is totally buried. There's barely room for me on the bed, let alone Ford.

The state of the room has kept me safe, like a protective nest.

I'd rather have Ford.

I toss Darby on the bed, then begin cleaning. I hang the clean clothes in the closet, put them in the drawers. I find trash bags, then pack up most of the stuffed animals and extra blankets, tossing the bags into the garage to get rid of later. I haul boxes of who knows what out to the garage too.

After a long time, the cleaning frenzy winds down. I stand in my room, my feet on carpet that I couldn't see earlier.

The room looks like it used to. Usable, clean.

I feel good—really good. Lighter somehow.

Sitting on the made bed, I look at Onyx and take a deep breath. "It's a start," I tell the cat.

I enjoy the room for a few minutes, then check the time. It's after eleven. Time to go to Dad's and release Elsa.

With a sudden shock, I realize that I never asked Dad if we could come over. My good mood vanishes.

Stupid of me.

I dial his number, and it takes several rings until he answers. When he does, I know I've woken him.

"Are you busy?" I ask.

"I'm sleeping, but that's okay. What's up?" he asks with a touch of concern.

I give him the run-down of what we need to do with Darby.

"Why here? Why not your house?"

I don't know how to explain it exactly, so I just say, "We need all the holy we can get. What better place than a pastor's house?"

He accepts this, bless him.

TWENTY-THREE

RYLAN FLYNN

I jam out to music on my way to Dad's, with Darby in the front seat next to me. As I belt out the words to "Grave Digger" by Matt Maeson, the bear begins to rock to the beat.

It makes me smile thinking Elsa is enjoying the music.

Soon she'll be free.

Ford, Mickey and Lorraine are not here yet. I take a moment to finish another listen of the song before turning the car off. The sudden silence and darkness of the cab is startling.

"I love you," Elsa squeaks, making me jump.

"I know, honey. I wish your mom and dad were here for this."

"Mommy?" A choked whisper.

Sitting sideways in the car so I have room, I pull the bear to my chest. The fur is still damp in places from my tears earlier.

I will miss this bear. Darby has been a good friend to me for the time I've had him.

But Elsa must be released, and I don't know any other way to do it.

With a tight squeeze, I say, "Thank you."

Someone knocks on my window, a gentle rap. Flowing

white fabric ripples in the darkness of the driveway—bangle bracelets jingle.

It's Lorraine the White Witch.

I climb out of the car with Darby in tow. "Thanks for coming," I tell her.

She scrutinizes the bear, looking into Darby's eyes. "I feel the energy from it. You were right to call me. There is definitely something inside," she says.

"Will burning the bear release the little girl?"

Lorraine touches Darby's arm, then pulls her hand away as if from something hot. "I think so. I read more about cases like this after we talked. The flames are cleansing."

"That was my thought too. I just don't want to do any damage to her spirit."

"Being trapped like this isn't good for her either. We can only try to help." Lorraine turns her attention to me. "Something's different with you. You seem lighter, despite what we're here to do."

I squirm under the intense scrutiny. "I... I have a boyfriend."

"That would do it."

Headlights pull up to the house—Mickey's car.

We meet her and her camera under the always-on porch light, just as Ford parks behind her car. I sit Darby on my hip and wait for Ford to join us.

"Ready for this, Elsa?" he asks.

"Daddy?" Elsa asks.

"She says hi," I tell him with a wry smile.

Lorraine watches with interest, then gives me a knowing look.

"This is so weird," Mickey says. "Even for us."

"I know. It's kind of breaking my heart," I say, knocking on the door before I open it. "Dad, we're here."

"Come on through," he calls from the kitchen. "I was just getting some sweet tea. Anyone want some?"

We all decline. Dad takes a long drink from his glass, eyeing Darby the whole time. "So this is the haunted bear?" he asks, setting the glass down by the sink.

"His name is Darby. Elsa White is inside him," I explain.

"God sure made an interesting world," he says, looking closely at Darby.

"Do you think burning the bear will release Elsa?" Ford asks the room.

Dad pulls his eyes away from Darby and seems to notice Ford for the first time. "Good to see you again, Ford. Been a while." They shake hands like old friends, then Dad shoots me a quick look that's full of questions.

I place a hand on Ford's shoulder, wordlessly answering him.

Dad nods with a twinkle in his eye. "I don't know much about possessed toys, but I'd think, once the bear is gone, the spirit will have to be released."

"I agree. Without the bear to inhabit, her spirit will have nothing to be tied to," Lorraine says.

Dad looks at Lorraine and reaches out his hand. "I don't think we've met. I'm Brett Flynn, Rylan's father. Rylan said you have some experience in these matters."

Lorraine's bracelets jingle as she shakes his hand. "Pleased to meet you. Yes, I have a lot of experience with the other worlds. It's what I do. Readings and potions and studying the occult. What do you do?"

"I'm a pastor."

"Interesting. You have experience of another world too, a different kind of magic."

Dad smiles at Lorraine. "I haven't thought of it that way before, but I guess you're right." He turns his attention back to Darby. "So, what happens once she's free of the bear?"

"I'd love to cross her tonight," I say, "but I'm pretty sure she wants to see her parents, and they're not at all receptive to the thought of ghosts, let alone to their daughter being one."

"Most people would be a little freaked at that," Mickey says. "I know I would be, if it was my daughter."

The big grandfather clock in the dining room strikes midnight—we fall silent as the chimes fill the house. Darby wiggles in my arms.

"I think she's ready," I say in a hushed voice.

Dad opens a drawer, taking out a long lighter and making sure it works. "This should do it."

"Do you have any lighter fluid?" I ask.

"It's out by the grill. We can do this in the firepit." Dad opens the back door, and we file out after him.

The back deck is dark, lit only by a tiny glimmer from the moon and the lights from the kitchen.

"Should I turn on the light?" Dad wonders.

"The dark is better," Lorraine says.

"Yeah, I'd keep it dark," Mickey says.

I approach the metal firepit at the far corner of the deck, holding the bear tight. Now that it's happening, I don't want to let Darby go.

"I know this is hard, but we have to think of Elsa," Ford tells me.

"I'm not sure why this is getting to me so much," I say.

"Because the bear was good company for you before," Mickey says. "I hate thinking of you all alone in that empty house. I'm glad you had him."

If she only knew how full my house really is.

"Wait," Dad says, "I forgot my Bible." He hurries back into the house.

Ford retrieves the lighter fluid from by the grill, and Mickey pats Darby on the head.

"Good luck," she says. I'm not sure if she means to Elsa or to me.

Dad returns with his Bible, and we surround the firepit. "I think we should start with a prayer," he says.

We all bow our heads and Dad begins. "Dear Lord, please bring your favor on this. Your child, Elsa, needs your help to release her soul. Please guide her and protect her journey. Amen."

We raise our heads.

"I guess it's time," I say. I step toward the large metal bowl, the remnants of past fires at the bottom, bits of coal and ash.

I hate to put Darby in the dirty pit, but what we're about to do to him is worse.

"It will be okay," Mickey says as she lifts the camera to her shoulder and turns it on.

"Goodbye, Darby," I say, placing the large bear in the bowl. He's so big that his legs stick out.

"Ready?" Ford asks, the bottle of lighter fluid at the ready.

"Do it," I say.

He squeezes the bottle and fluid sprays all over the bear. The chemical smell fills the deck.

When he's done, he steps back. "Who wants to light it?" he asks.

"I think Rylan should," Dad says, opening the Bible. "I'll read as you do it."

"And I'll say some chants I looked up for the occasion," Lorraine adds.

I take the stick lighter and approach. Lorraine is chanting to the sky, her hands raised to the stars. Dad is reading a passage I recognize from Psalms, his head bowed reverently. Saying my own silent prayer—that this works, that Elsa can find some peace—I click the lighter.

The flames whoosh into life.

Darby's mostly plastic fur instantly begins to melt.

Mickey says from behind the camera. "Lord, please let this work."

Darby is in flames, the burning plastic smell stinging my nose.

Dad continues reading, his voice growing more excited.

Lorraine continues chanting, her flowing dress swaying as she waves her arms rhythmically.

"Come on, Elsa," Ford says. "You can do this."

A glow that's not from the fire fills what's left of Darby.

"I can see her light," I say. "I think it's working."

"Mommy!" Elsa shouts as the light separates and rises into the air. The light takes the form of a little girl.

"She's free! She did it!" I shout, tears streaming down my cheeks. "I can see her."

Elsa floats, stretching her arms out wide in wonder. "I'm me," she says.

"You're you," I tell her.

My words startle her. She suddenly looks around the deck, over the dark yard to the horizon, obviously frightened.

"You're okay now," I tell her.

She only glances at me, then fades into the dark.

"Elsa, come back!" I shout.

"What happened?" Ford asks.

Dad stops reading. Lorraine falls silent.

"She just left. She came out and just faded away." My voice rises in panic.

"Where would she go?" Ford asks.

"To her parents' house maybe? How would she know the way?" I ask.

"Should we go after her?" Mickey asks.

"I don't know." I look to Dad. "What do you think?"

"What will you do if you find her? You said she wanted to see her parents. She'll find them. God will guide her."

Lorraine adds, "She has a journey of her own to make now."

What's left of Darby sizzles in the firepit. The tips of his feet still poke past the rim of the bowl. Disappointed, and a bit disgusted with myself, I push them into the fire, watching them light.

"I should have stopped her from leaving. Now she's all alone again."

"You can't control the spirits, you can only guide them," Ford says reasonably.

Mickey turns off the camera and lowers it. "You did all you could," she says.

I know they all mean well, but I still feel awful.

Dad closes the Bible and puts an arm around my shoulder. "You did good, Rylan. You really did."

"I hope it's enough. Maybe she'll come back."

We don't say anything else as we watch Darby disintegrate. As he turns into melted black ashes, my mood plummets.

Dad stirs the remnants with a metal poker. "Looks like he's gone."

"Poor Darby," I say, pulling my leather jacket tighter around me.

I want to go home.

"We've done what we could for tonight," Ford says, pulling me against his chest. I lean into him, breathing in his scent. It helps a little, but I still feel miserable.

"Her spirit will find its way," Lorraine says.

"Let's go," I say. We don't leave through the house; we just say goodbye to Dad and walk around to the front.

I have no words left, so I just wave goodbye and get into my car, leaving the others to watch me drive away.

I'm halfway home when I decide to look for Elsa. I drive to her parents' house, searching the dark for a glowing child.

I park in front of their house. It's dark, not even a porch light.

Should I tell them what happened?

Would that just increase their grief?

Nothing moves in their neighborhood, and I eventually grow sleepy waiting for Elsa.

Sad and disappointed, I return home.

As I let myself in the back door, I hear something I haven't heard in a long time.

Mom is laughing.

I hurry to her door and look inside.

Mom is sitting on the bed with Elsa by her side. They are laughing and talking, and they don't seem to realize I'm there.

I soak in the fact that Elsa is safe, and that Mom is happy.

I don't interrupt, just go to bed in my clean room. I fall asleep with the sound of their laughter in my ears.

TWENTY-FOUR

TYLER SPENCER

I look across my desk to where Ford would normally be sitting. This morning, his desk is empty. I miss my friend and my partner. I'd love to talk over what we've found out with him, but the chief was adamant.

"Can't risk this not standing up in court," he said.

I can only hope we get that far. I don't have a solid suspect besides Eli. With his young face and simple clothes, he doesn't look like a violent person. I'm not naïve enough to think an innocent-looking man could never be a killer, but my gut tells me he's not our guy. Which means the killer is still out there somewhere.

My phone rings, breaking my moment of contemplation.

"Hey, Tyler, this is Doris down in dispatch."

"Good morning, Doris. What's up?"

"I just got a call you'd be interested in. Someone says they saw your victim with a man on the night she was killed."

"Interesting." I grab a pen, ready to write down every detail. "Did they say who the man was?"

"Not exactly, but get this. They said he was Amish. They were riding in a buggy together."

"A buggy here in Ashby?"

"Not here, but near the bridge where you found your girl."

My heart sinks. Eli. It has to be Eli. "Did they give a description of the man?"

"Young man in dark clothes, no beard. That's all they really remembered. They all dress alike."

I rub my temple. "Thank you, Doris."

"Hope the tip helps."

I hang up, a dread mounting in my chest. I lean back in my chair and look at the ceiling.

Eli Graber. It has to be.

My cell phone chirps, and I see a text from the lab.

The DNA found in Kenzie matches Eli.

I was wrong about him—so wrong. The innocent-looking young man is actually a brutal killer.

The office door suddenly opens and Faith breezes in.

"Sorry I'm late. Halle wasn't feeling well, and it took a lot to convince her to go to school. Probably should have kept her home, but I know you needed me today." She stops suddenly, studies my face. "What's happened?" She sets her purse on Ford's desk.

"Two things actually. The DNA is Eli's, and we just got a tip that someone matching his description was seen driving Kenzie in a buggy near our crime scene on the night she was killed."

Faith's shoulders slump. "So he's guilty."

"Looks like it."

"Let's go get him." She snatches her purse with excitement.

"It's not that easy."

"Why not? Because you don't want it to be him? Look, I'm telling you, the facts all lead to him, not to mention statistics."

"I don't care about statistics, I just feel we're missing something here. Why would Eli cut her hip like that? Doesn't make sense."

"Murder never makes sense. He has motive and means and now we know he had the opportunity. What else do you want?"

"What motive?"

"I don't know much about the Amish, but don't they frown on dating outside of their people? As the apparent heir to the furniture factory, wouldn't that be even more reason not to go outside of the order? Kenzie was a liability."

"I just don't see him doing it." I don't know why I'm debating it. Faith is right, and we've taken in suspects on less.

"Don't let the clothes and the lifestyle fool you. He may be Amish, but he's still just a person. People do horrible things to each other all the time."

She's right. I know she's right.

"I'll call for the warrant," I say, reluctantly picking up the phone.

Faith and I drive out to the country for Eli. I wanted to call the factory to be sure he was there, but didn't want to tip them off that we were coming.

"Think he's at work?" Faith asks as we drive. "Maybe we should try his farm."

"It's a weekday afternoon. The factory is our best bet."

"Yeah, maybe." She looks over the warrant in her hand. "I just hope there isn't any trouble with the dad and grandpa."

"Me too. Or the other men that work there."

"Maybe we should have brought backup?"

"Let's just see how it goes." I park in the same place we did last time. Black buggies and brown horses are still parked at the far end. Only a few cars are parked on this end.

"How do you want to play this?" Faith asks. "Just walk in all casual? Or rush in and take him by surprise?"

I watch a horse lift its head and look at us. Beyond the horse is a field, freshly planted. An arrest for murder seems so foreign in this place.

"I think casual is the way to go," I say without much enthusiasm.

"What's the problem?" Faith asks, not unkindly. "You act like you don't want to do this."

"I still feel like we're missing something. Once we go in there, this young man's life will never be the same."

"He made that choice when he took Kenzie's life. She has no say anymore. We are here for her. Remember that."

She's right, and I know it.

"If you need encouragement, just picture Kenzie being held underwater with this boy's hands around her neck."

The image makes me shiver inside. I look away from the horses and the field. "You're right," I say with more confidence. "Let's go take him in."

The woman in the showroom is looking at us from the window as we walk across the gravel parking lot, no doubt drawn by the cruiser we drove this time. It has a cage in back. She hurries to meet us when we enter.

"You're back," she says, running her hand nervously down her dress skirt. "This isn't about Eli, is it?"

"Where is he?" Faith asks, taking control.

Her eyes dart to the door leading to the workshop.

"Thank you," Faith says, marching to the door.

I follow, thinking of Kenzie, thinking of duty, thinking we don't belong here.

"Eli Graber," Faith shouts as we crush through the shop door and head toward the lathes where he's working.

"Yes?" He turns, his face full of fear.

"We have a warrant for your arrest," she says, waving the paper.

"Arrest for what?" Grandpa Elisha hurries across the shop.

"For the murder of Mackenzie Odell," I say, stepping up next to Faith.

Elisha takes the paper and reads over it. "Is this real?"

"Do we look like we're joking?" Faith asks.

"Now, Eli, don't give us any hassle and we'll make this easy on you," I say.

Eli takes a step back toward the lathe that's still running. He's still holding a chisel—a potential weapon.

"Can you put that down?" I ask sternly.

He places the chisel on the work bench, and I relax just a little.

"You can't take my son," Aaron says with authority as he turns off the machine.

"We have a warrant," Faith says.

"I don't care about your warrant. You can't take him." Aaron addresses me, not Faith.

"We can and we are." I take out my handcuffs and reach for Eli. "Please turn around."

Eli's eyes are huge. He looks desperately to his father and grandfather for help.

"We'll figure this out," Elisha says.

Aaron tries to get between us.

"Don't interfere, or we'll take you in too," I tell him.

"Eli Graber, you are under arrest for the murder of Mackenzie Odell," Faith begins.

Eli turns around and I place the cuffs on him. "I don't understand," he pleads.

"We had a tip that you were seen with her in your buggy near the bridge the night she was killed. Plus, your DNA was found in her."

"I wasn't near any bridge, and I already explained about the DNA. It was from the night before," he says desperately.

"You have the right to remain silent," Faith continues.

"I'd never hurt Kenzie!" Eli is shouting as we lead him from the shop. "Please don't do this."

It hurts to listen to his pleading, but I picture Kenzie's pale body on the lab table. "You should have thought of that before you strangled her."

"I didn't—"

"Save it," Faith says, shoving him out the shop door, into the showroom. Aaron and Elisha follow, begging us to let him go.

"We can't. We have a warrant to serve," I explain.

A few customers are in the showroom, watching us with open interest.

"You can't let them take me," Eli pleads with his family.

"Don't worry, son. We'll figure this out," Elisha says, following us out the front door.

"When can we see him?" Aaron asks.

"He'll be held until his arraignment, then booked into the county jail until trial. You can see him when he gets to county," Faith says.

"Trial? Oh, Lord, help us," Aaron says. "Be strong, boy."

We tuck Eli into the backseat of the cruiser, as he continues protesting his innocence. Faith and I hurriedly get in and drive out of the parking lot. Elisha, Aaron and what must be the whole crew of the shop watch us drive away.

"You have this all wrong," Eli says from the backseat.

He turns his attention from us and begins to pray.

I pray too. Pray we're not making a huge mistake.

TWENTY-FIVE

RYLAN FLYNN

The house is quiet when I wake up. Too quiet.

I sit up, disoriented by my clean room.

"Elsa?" I call.

Still quiet.

I hurry down the hall to Mom's room and look inside. The room is empty.

"Mom? Elsa?" I call down the hall. Did I lose the little girl again?

Onyx sits near his bowl in the kitchen and meows, giving me attitude. I absently feed him, wondering where Elsa has gone. Mom comes and goes from here to somewhere I've never asked about. Did Elsa go to that same place?

Will she come back?

I feel responsible for the girl. She was sort of safe inside Darby—now she could be in danger.

I think of the thing locked down the hall and run to the pile of boxes.

"Elsa, are you in there?"

I hear a snarl, but no Elsa.

Backing away, I decide I'd better go look for her. Maybe she went home.

Soon I'm parked in front of her parents' house again, watching for a shimmer of a little girl.

I see one on a bike down the block, but she's dark-haired and Elsa is a blonde.

It's not her. Just a girl out playing.

I don't know where else to look for her. I'm not even sure how she found my house last night.

Elsa's mom, Rochelle, comes out front, staring at my car.

I try for casual, like I'm supposed to be parked in the street in front of her house, but she doesn't buy it. She storms across the yard toward me.

Rochelle knocks on the passenger window, and I reach over to roll it down.

"What are you doing here?" she demands. "I saw this huge old car parked here last night. I know who you are. You're that ghost lady coming to torture me again with your lies."

"I don't want to torture you. I just need you to know the truth about your daughter."

"Elsa is dead. You can't bring her back."

"Her spirit is still here. She was locked inside the giant bear I bought from you."

Her face grows dark. "Why are you doing this? Can't you leave us alone?"

"Elsa wants you. She wants to tell you she loves you. Maybe then she can cross over."

"She's dead. She's already dead. Now leave us alone!"

Rochelle pulls away from the window and crosses her arms.

"I'm just trying to help."

"You're not helping. Now leave before I call the police and have you arrested for harassment."

"I've seen Elsa. She's free of the bear. We released her last night."

"If she's free of the bear, where is she?" she asks sarcastically. "I don't see her."

"I don't know. I'd hoped she'd come here."

"So you lost her? How convenient. Now go away. I've heard enough."

Rochelle's face is set. There's no convincing her.

With nothing else to do, I start the car and drive away.

I don't know where to go and just cruise the area near Elsa's house for a while. As I drive, I grow desperate looking for her.

Rochelle was right about one thing—I lost Elsa.

The enormity of the situation weighs on me. A little girl's spirit is floating around town, untethered and vulnerable.

I stop by the house, hoping against hope she's returned.

The house is still quiet. No Elsa. No Mom.

There's nothing else to do but pray. I drop to my knees in the kitchen and bow my head. I pray for Elsa's safe return and for all the spirits that roam Ashby.

It doesn't feel like enough.

I need a bigger prayer.

I run to my car and drive the few blocks to Dad's church—all the while, searching for any sign of Elsa.

The small cemetery by the church is peaceful in the late morning sun. I bow my head and hurry past the stones, trying not to be noticed by the spirits I've seen here before.

Taking the steps two at a time, I rush into the church.

Inside, it's dim and cool.

And serene.

I hear Dad on the phone in his office, but that's not why I'm here.

I need guidance that only God can give.

Slowly opening the door to the sanctuary, I step into the room. The empty pews stretch out from the center aisle, and I silently pass them. I stare up at the cross behind the pulpit, rapt with feeling. Dropping to my knees at the altar, I bow my head, clasping my hands in front of my chest.

"Dear God," I start, "I need you. I've lost one of your souls and I can't find her. I was only trying to help. I'm always trying to help, but I messed up."

My voice breaks. Tears sting my eyes.

I squeeze them shut tight and continue.

"Lord, please protect Elsa. Please look after Mom. Please guide me as I try to do Your work to help souls reach You."

I stop to breathe, to feel His presence.

I hear a tiny giggle far across the room.

My head snaps up as I open my eyes.

"I like that," a small voice whispers. "Are you looking for me?"

It's Elsa, sitting in the corner of the church, watching.

Next to her is Mom.

"Where have you been?" I ask miserably. "I've been worried sick about you both."

"Elsa wanted to see the town. I wanted to check on your father. Even though we're divorced, I still worry. I wanted to make sure he's okay," Mom says.

"But... I don't understand. How did you get here?"

"Rylan, we're ghosts. We can go where we want." Mom's words shock me.

"I didn't think you knew you were a ghost. I thought—well, I don't know what I thought."

Mom takes Elsa's hand and leads her to me. "I only just realized. I've seen this." She points to the hole behind her ear, the mess of brains and flesh. "Once Elsa came to the house, I put it together."

"Can we go home now?" Elsa says.

"Home like my house, or home to your parents?" I ask.

"I tried to talk to my parents. That's where we went first. They can't see or hear me. You can."

"I really need to cross you over. I'm responsible for you."

"Please don't cross her," Mom says unexpectedly. "I like having her around."

"I can't keep her here. I have a duty to her and to God."

"But you haven't crossed me yet," Mom points out. "She can stay with me. She won't be any trouble." Mom's face pleads.

How can I say no?

"Maybe for a little while." I feel like I'm agreeing to let her have a pet.

"Yay!" Elsa says. "I like Miss Margie."

The door to the sanctuary opens and Dad walks in. "Hey, Rylan. I thought I heard a voice in here. Who are you talking to?" Dad looks around the pews.

"Elsa is here," I tell him. I don't mention Mom, of course.

"Here? How did that happen?"

"It's a long story," I hedge. "Thanks again for your help last night. I think Elsa will be okay now."

"Are you going to cross her over tonight? I can help."

Elsa and Mom are both shaking their heads.

"Not tonight. I still need her parents to be part of it. They aren't ready yet."

"Do you want me to talk to them?"

"Can we go now?" Elsa pouts.

"I'll talk to them again after a while. It's a lot to take in that a loved one's spirit is still here."

I glance at Mom. Should I tell Dad she's here too? Would he understand?

"Dad, I—"

"Time to go," Mom interrupts, reading my intention. "I've seen Brett and he's fine. Now let's get this girl home."

"Never mind," I finish. I hug Dad hard, soaking in the comfort only a father can give. "Thanks for all you do," I tell him.

"Are you okay, Rylan? You didn't tell me why you or Elsa are here."

"Let's just say I needed to talk to God, and Elsa was drawn here for her own reasons."

Dad shakes his head. "Always something mysterious with you."

"I try," I tease. "I'll see you later."

Mom and Elsa are already out the door, and I follow behind.

"Wait," he says. "I wanted to tell you I'm happy for you and Ford. Looks like you're getting along especially well. Does that mean what I think it means?"

I can't help smiling. "Yes."

"Good for you two," Dad says. "I've always liked that young man."

I wave goodbye and leave the church. A few ghosts shimmer in the ancient cemetery, but I don't look at them as I hurry to my car. Mom and Elsa have already disappeared. I feel a little left out. Mom has only had me since she died—now she and Elsa will have each other.

"Looks like I have a little sister," I tell myself as I drive away.

TWENTY-SIX
RYLAN FLYNN

With Elsa safely under Mom's care, I'm free to turn my mind to Kenzie's murder. I crank the music up loud in my car and drive aimlessly around town, thinking on what Hazel said about the young man who hung himself on the bridge. If he was a friend of Kenzie's, it has to be connected. It's too much of a coincidence, and I don't believe in coincidences. Especially not when it comes to murder.

I sit at a stop sign and wait for an oncoming car to go when a woman power-walking waves at me from the next corner. It takes me a moment to realize it's Delia, Ford's grandma. I pull over next to her on the curb.

"I thought that was you, Rylan," Delia says as I roll the window down. "Want to walk with me?"

I'm taken aback by her request, but her engaging smile pulls me out of the car. "Sure."

She holds a small pink weight in each hand. "I do this everyday that I can get out," she says as we start down the block, pumping the weights with her steps.

For a woman in her seventies, she's very fit—I have a hard time keeping up.

She notices and slows her pace.

"Sorry, I don't exercise much," I explain. "At least not like this."

"Keeps me young," she says, barely out of breath. "That's not why I asked you to join me."

"You want to ask about Ford and me."

She looks at me with new appreciation. "Yes, dear, I do. He's very special, as I'm sure you're aware."

"He's special to me too. You have no idea."

She stops walking and looks me in the eye. "You're in love with him, aren't you?"

I'm taken aback by the directness of her question, but I see only care and concern in her eyes, so I take the leap.

"I do love him. I've always loved him."

Delia studies me, taking stock. I must have passed her test—she's smiling as she says, "Welcome to the family," then continues walking.

"So how are you coming on solving my granddaughter's murder?"

"We're working on it, but honestly, I have no idea who hurt her. I'm sorry."

"Don't be sorry. It's great that you're helping. Too bad you can't just talk to her ghost and ask her what happened."

"That would be great, but it never seems to work out that way. There's a ghost on the bridge where Kenzie was found, but Hazel hasn't been much help. She did lead me to Kenzie, though, so I'm grateful for that. But she wasn't there the night Kenzie was killed, so she didn't see anything."

"Wasn't there? I thought ghosts were tied to where they died."

"Not always. They can travel sometimes, and they often disappear, at least from me."

"Where do they go?"

"I have no idea. I wish I did."

We round the corner of the block, and I see my car at the end.

"So, what's your best guess on what happened to Kenzie?" Delia pushes, a slight desperation in her voice.

"Hazel said a teenager hung himself there two years ago. He was a friend of Kenzie's. Seems like it must be connected."

"Oh, I remember that. Kenzie was really shaken up after. That's a big part of why she had to drop out of college. She tried, but, as I recall, she couldn't get over the shock of the suicide. Now, what was his name?"

"Miles," I supply.

"Oh yeah, Miles Crandall. I sold his parents their house a while before the tragedy. I remember seeing him at the showings. He didn't seem depressed or anything. A bit quiet, and he dressed a little darker than I like, but you know, kids. They like to think they're being different, but I've seen a lot in my years, and they're all the same in the end. Just scared inside."

"Do you think he could have been so scared that he hung himself?"

"I think we all have demons hiding."

I nearly trip in surprise but catch myself. I have something evil quite literally hiding in my house. I know that's not what she meant, but it shakes me a little anyway.

We've reached my car. Delia drops her pink weights to her side, takes a deep breath.

"Thanks for the walk," she says, then suddenly pulls me against her thin frame, the weights pushing into my back as she hugs. "I like you, Rylan Flynn."

"I like you too," I say, flustered.

"Will you be at the funeral tomorrow?"

"Ford hasn't asked me yet, but I'll most likely be there. What time?"

"Two."

"Then I can come. I have to do *The Bill and Frank Show* in

the morning, on the radio. They want to talk to me and Mickey, my best friend and camera person, about our show."

"That's wonderful! So your show is doing well? I watched some episodes after you visited. It's really interesting what you do. Especially that last one with the little boy and his mom."

"That one has really gotten a lot of views. It's kind of cool, what's going on with it."

"Well, congratulations. You deserve the success. Enjoy the show, and I'll see you at the funeral."

Delia waves a pink weight goodbye and walks away.

I watch her go, hoping I'm in such good shape when I'm her age.

I'd left my phone in the car on my impromptu walk and have a missed text from Ford.

Three words that make my heart sing.

They got him.

TWENTY-SEVEN

RYLAN FLYNN

I quickly call Ford back. "What do you mean 'they got him'? Who was it?"

"You won't believe it. They just arrested Eli," he says.

"Eli? You're right, I don't believe it. How did they catch him?"

"Tyler just called to tell me they took him in today. His DNA was in her body, and they had a tip that an Amish man fitting his description was seen with her the night she died."

"That's pretty damning evidence. Holy flip, Eli? Now that's a shock."

"Not really. It's usually the significant other. Just statistically speaking, it was likely him."

"So, what do we do now?" I'm half-afraid he won't want to see me without a case to work on.

"Want to come over for dinner? I have some steaks I can put on the grill."

"To your apartment?" I've never been to his place before.

"Sure, why not? I'd love to see you." I can't miss the note of suggestion in his voice. It warms my heart.

I look down at my T-shirt, sweaty from the walk with Delia. "I need to go home and change first."

"Okay, but don't take too long."

I normally only wear T-shirts and skinny jeans, but it feels like tonight calls for something a little nicer. This will be our first "date," if you want to call it that. I should at least dress in clean clothes.

I search my newly organized closet for a soft pink top with ruffled short sleeves I used to wear to church. It takes some searching, but I finally find the top squeezed between a sweater and a tank top, all the way at the end of the rack.

The top thankfully doesn't have any stains, and it smells okay. After how I've been just throwing things on the chair in my room, I'm not surprised to see it's wrinkled, but it'll have to do.

I pull it on and check myself in the mirror. The shade of pink goes well with my light brown hair and blue eyes. I feel almost pretty.

And brave.

I dig even deeper in the closet and come up with a knee-length jean skirt. After a good brushing of my hair and a little makeup, I barely recognize the woman in the mirror.

Now I just need shoes. My usual black Chuck Taylors will not do.

No matter how I search, I can't find the sandals I have in mind. They've been lost to the hoard. Having nothing else to wear, I decide to go barefoot.

Ford will hopefully think it's cute.

The hungry look in his eye when he answers the door tells me he's not thinking of my bare feet. He makes it look casual, but I can tell he's checking out my legs.

I feel deliciously exposed in this skirt.

Ford is dressed in a maroon checked short-sleeve button-down and dark jeans. I'm glad to see he dressed for dinner too.

"You look great," he says, leading me inside his apartment.

"So do you." My belly swirls with nerves at being alone like this. It feels different, like something has shifted between us.

Ford seems completely at ease as he offers me a drink. "I have wine."

"I'd love a glass." I stand by the kitchen island as he pours white wine in two glasses, then hands me one.

"Seriously, Rylan. You look amazing."

"I had to change. I got all sweaty from power-walking with your grandma." I take a sip of the wine. It's sweet and tangy, just like I like it.

"Grandma Delia? How did that come about?"

"I was driving near her neighborhood, and she flagged me down. She wanted to check me out, I think."

Ford's eyes twinkle in mirth. "She did? Sounds like her. How did you do?"

"Good, I think. She said 'welcome to the family' and gave me a hug. That has to be good, right?"

"Wow! For Grandma, that's really good." He sits his wine glass down and picks up a platter with two steaks on it. "You hungry? I have the grill hot."

"I'm starving." Besides a quick peanut-butter sandwich earlier, I haven't eaten.

"Let's go out on the patio," he says, pushing open the sliding door. "Bring the wine."

I grab the bottle and follow him outside, then sit at the glass table. Soon the air is full of the scent of grilling meat.

I'm not sure what to say, so I take another sip of the sweet wine. I don't want to talk about the case. I don't want to talk about work.

"This is kind of weird, isn't it?" he asks, taking the seat next to me. "Weird and wonderful."

"I was thinking the same thing. It's like a first date, all awkward, but we've known each other for years."

"I kind of like it." His eyes trail over my lips—I know he wants to kiss me.

"I like it too." I lick my lips nervously. He pulls his eyes away.

"If this was a regular first date, I'd say tell me about your childhood, but since I was there for a lot of it, that doesn't really apply."

"But I don't know about yours, besides that you've been friends with Keaton forever and were always around. Tell me something I don't know."

Ford leans back in his chair, taking a sip of wine. "Something you don't know? Let's see. I almost got kicked out of the police academy. I bet you didn't know that."

My eyes fly wide. "You? I don't believe it. What did you do?"

"I actually didn't do anything. A guy I bunked with got ahold of some pot and, when he got caught with it, he said I sold it to him. I didn't of course, but my dreams were almost crushed. They figured out he was lying and I was off the hook, but that was too close for me."

"That would have been awful. What would you have done instead?"

"That's the thing. I had no backup plan. I always knew I wanted to be an officer. Always pictured myself as a detective, maybe chief one day."

"Chief Pierce. That sounds good."

He returns to the grill and flips the steaks. "How about you? What did you want to be when you grew up?"

"Oh, well, I never had a grand plan like you. My life is a little complicated with the ghosts and all. It was Mickey's idea to make the show. I'm so glad she did."

"You worked at that doctor's office for a while."

"That was just a receptionist job. It paid the bills, but it wasn't what I'd call a career choice."

"And now the show pays the bills?" he asks.

"Luckily, my bills are pretty minimal since I inherited Mom's house. Actually, the show is doing amazing right now. Mickey and I are going to be on *The Bill and Frank Show* tomorrow morning."

"That's great! You should get lots of publicity from that."

"I just hope they don't make fun of me. They're known for making fun of guests, and everyone else for that matter."

"You'll do fine." He takes the steaks off the grill and sits the platter in front of me. "You sit right there, and I'll bring everything else out. It's just salad and some bread. I hope that's okay."

"Sounds wonderful, but I'll help."

I jump from my seat before he can argue. Soon the table is set and we're ready to eat. I pick up my fork.

"Do you mind if I say a prayer first?" he asks.

I set my fork down, impressed. "Please do."

He takes my hand and bows his head. "Dear Lord, thank You for this meal and thank You for Your many blessings. Thank You for the company." He squeezes my hand. "Amen."

"That was lovely," I say, not wanting to let go of his fingers. There's a fire burning where our skin touches.

"Eat up," he says, kissing my fingers before letting them go.

"Looks amazing," I say, a little breathlessly, not sure if I mean the food or the man.

The nervous jitters disappear as we eat dinner. We soon find ourselves laughing and reminiscing like the old friends we are.

But we're more than friends now. The slight crackle in the air between us is proof of that.

Long after dinner, we sit on the patio. As the sun sets behind the trees, we fall quiet. The wine is gone, the food is gone. I'm happy and relaxed, but an expectant tension swirls around us.

After several minutes of companionable silence, Ford pushes his chair back from the table. "I should get this inside before it's fully dark," he says of the plates.

I help carry the empties into the kitchen, placing them by the sink.

"I'll wash those later," he says, stepping behind me.

"I can do them now," I offer half-heartedly, feeling the heat of him being so close.

"Do you really want to do dishes?" he whispers near my ear, sending shivers down my arm.

"I can think of something else we can do." I press my back to his chest as he wraps his arms around my waist, pulling me close.

I pull my hair to the side, giving him access to my neck. He accepts the invitation eagerly, his lips driving my tender skin wild.

"Will you stay?" he asks.

"You couldn't make me leave." I turn in his arms and kiss him hard. He kisses me back, moaning against my mouth.

When he finally pulls away, he takes my hand and leads me down a hall. It's dark, but he doesn't turn on the lights until we reach his room. Then he only turns on a lamp—the room is bathed in soft light.

Anticipation burns in my blood as he wraps me in his arms again, molding himself to me.

My mind can barely believe this is happening after years of wishing.

My body responds to his touch, and the feeling surprises me with its intensity.

I unbutton his shirt, exposing chest hair and muscles that I run a palm over. He moans gently at my touch, pulling me close.

The pink blouse is too much between us. I start to pull it over my head—he helps me.

He takes a moment to look at me, his face full of desire.

While he watches, I unhook my bra slowly and drop it to the floor. He touches me softly, running his palm across my bare skin.

It drives me wild.

Desire burns inside me, and I pull him to the bed.

The lamp is still on much later when I wake in Ford's arms. He feels me shift and tightens his arm around me, not waking up. I snuggle closer, fitting my head against his bare chest.

It feels right. Familiar.

I press my body against the full length of him, enjoying the skin-on-skin contact. He's warm in his sleep.

I'm happier than I ever remember being. Fulfilled in a way I didn't imagine was possible.

This is my man. This is my person.

He breathes deeply, evenly. At peace.

I run my fingers through his chest hair, drifting.

The words come to my tongue unbidden. I whisper, "I love you, Ford," into the quiet.

"I love you, Rylan," he mumbles back, not actually awake.

They are the sweetest words I've ever heard. Made all the more precious as he doesn't know he's said them.

Tears of happiness sting my eyes as I press my face to the side of his chest.

The moment is perfect. The night was perfect.

I reach for the lamp and click it off.
Ford rolls to his side and pulls my back against his chest.
I've never slept so well in my life.

TWENTY-EIGHT

RYLAN FLYNN

It takes a moment to realize the thing under my neck is an arm. I open my eyes and see an unfamiliar room. Images of last night flood my mind when I realize where I am and who I'm with.

It wasn't a dream.

It happened.

My sleepy mind registers music playing—a familiar tune.

I sit up suddenly, realizing it's Mickey's ringtone on my phone. Ford stirs next to me, "What's wrong?"

"I think I'm late." I toss the covers back, then quickly pull them over me again.

I'm naked under the bedspread.

Ford watches from his side of the bed. "Don't cover yourself for my sake. I like what I'm seeing," he teases as the phone stops ringing.

Last night, I had no problem losing my clothes. This morning, I'm shy, nervous. All of this is so new, I'm not sure how to act.

"I'm sorry," I hold the covers to my chest. "I'm just—"

He reaches for my hand. "Don't apologize. I understand." He gets out of bed, his bare backside in sight until he pulls on a pair of boxer briefs. I have to agree, I like what I see too. His body is muscled in all the right places.

I can't believe he's standing in the same room with me, nearly undressed. I'm tempted to throw off the blankets and invite him back to bed.

But the phone rings again and I remember where I'm supposed to be this morning.

The radio station.

"Can you find my phone? I think it's in my skirt pocket."

Ford fishes the phone out and hands it to me.

"Where are you?" Mickey shouts. "You are so late."

"I'm—" I don't know what to tell her.

"I'll go make coffee," Ford whispers and leaves the room.

"You're not home, I went by to pick you up like you said yesterday and your car wasn't there. I thought you went to the station, but you're not here either." Mickey's talking so fast, I can't get a word in.

As I listen, I'm shimmying into my clothes.

When she stops to take a breath, I say, "I'll be right there. I'm sorry," and hang up.

I run from the bedroom into the kitchen where Ford is standing by the sink, still in his underwear.

Man, he looks good.

"I have to go," I say, looking for shoes, then remembering I didn't wear any. "I was supposed to meet Mickey to do *The Bill and Frank Show* this morning."

"You're leaving?" Ford sounds a little put out.

"I'm so sorry. I should have set an alarm, but I got distracted," I tease, trying to soften the blow. "I'll make it up to you."

He hands me a coffee in a to-go cup. "Cream and sugar, right?"

I take the coffee gratefully. "You're the best," I tell him.

"You still coming to the funeral later?"

"Wouldn't miss it."

"Good luck on the show. I'll be listening."

I kiss him on the cheek and hurry out the door.

Mickey paces in front of the studio, watching the drive for me.

I park quickly and run across the pavement in my bare feet, wishing I had shoes, any shoes. Mickey looks over my rumpled pink frilly shirt and jean skirt, her eyes lingering on my lack of footwear.

"Trying out a new look?" she teases, holding open the door to the studio. "I mean, you look pretty, but not your usual self."

"I didn't have time to change."

"Ah, now I get it. You didn't sleep at home last night." She throws me a huge smile. "I'm so happy for you two."

I feel myself blush but manage to mumble a thank you before we're met by a producer.

"From *Beyond the Dead*?" the producer asks. "Mickey and Rylan, right?"

"That's us," Mickey says.

"I've seen your show. Good stuff. We don't have much time to go over things."

"I know, we're a bit late. I'm sorry about that," I say.

"Just be yourselves and don't take anything they say personally. It's all for the show. Bill and Frank are actually really nice guys. They love your work, so this should be easy." The producer leads us past the window to the studio, where Bill and Frank are wearing headphones and talking to each other. "Just about commercial time," she says. "Then we'll go in."

She barely finishes the sentence when they break for commercial. She leads us into the studio.

Mickey and I take the seats across from Bill and Frank and put on headphones the producer offers.

"The ghost hunters," Bill is saying. "Nice of you to finally join us." There's a twinkle in his eye.

"Making a dramatic entrance," Frank says. "Seriously, though. Nice of you to join us."

My nerves are jumping, and my chest feels tight. I can't believe we're doing this. I wish I hadn't been late so I had some time to settle in before going on the air. I sit up straight and take a deep breath.

"Don't be nervous," Bill says. "We'll take it easy on you." He winks.

I'm conscious of the seconds ticking away, wishing I'd never agreed to this.

Mickey catches my eye—she looks as scared as me. "We got this," she says.

The producer steps out of the room, leaving us alone with the DJs and one other woman with extremely pale hair. I don't know what her job is, but she makes no move to leave and doesn't put on headphones. She seems completely uninterested in what's going on.

"Welcome back to *The Bill and Frank Show*," Bill is saying —we're on air. "We have a real treat today. The ladies from the hit YouTube show *Beyond the Dead* are here in the studio with us. Rylan Flynn and Mickey Ramirez."

Bill looks at us, waiting for a reply.

"Hello, thanks for having us," Mickey says into the microphone. I say the same thing. My voice sounds high and strange to my ears.

"Which of you is the ghost hunter?" Frank asks.

"That's me," I say. "Rylan."

"And you actually see ghosts, Rylan? You can talk to them?" Frank asks.

The woman lingering in the studio suddenly looks at me.

"Yes, I do." I don't know what else to say.

"For any of our listeners who haven't seen the show, it's mostly Rylan talking to ghosts on film," Mickey says, saving me. "Sometimes, she helps the spirits cross over."

"As in over to the other side. Into heaven?" Bill asks.

"That's what I believe," I say. The strange woman is openly staring at me, walking closer. No one is paying her any attention.

"You've seen it? Seen heaven?" Frank asks.

"I've seen a light, and the spirits go into the light. I don't know where they go, but I like to think it's heaven."

"That's fascinating," Bill says.

The woman pushes up right next to me. "You can see me, can't you?" she asks.

With a sinking feeling, I realize the tingle in my back isn't just from nerves.

"Do you see ghosts a lot?" Frank asks. "Are there that many ghosts in Ashby?"

"You'd be surprised how many places are what you'd call haunted," Mickey says. "We get a lot of calls locally."

"I've always thought this building was haunted," Frank says. "Sometimes, I hear things. Is that what you mean?"

I'm trying to ignore the woman next to me and focus on the show, but the woman won't stop pestering me.

"You can see me, I know you can. Can you help me like you said you help the others?"

Bill and Frank are looking at me, waiting for a response.

Mickey steps in again. "Sometimes, it's noises we investigate; sometimes, it's things moving, or just a cold place in a building."

The woman's face grows serious—she looks like she's concentrating.

Although the studio is fully enclosed, a cool breeze presses against my skin.

Bill and Frank look at each other but continue the show.

"When did you first realize you could see ghosts? Were you born that way?" Bill asks.

"When I was a kid, I fell through the ice on a pond and

nearly froze to death," I tell him. "I saw the light for the first time. After that, I started seeing shadows and misty shapes. It grew stronger, and now I can see them clearly wherever I go."

Bill rubs goosebumps on his arms. "Do you all feel that? It's getting cold in here."

The woman is now waving her arms and shouting. "Help me cross over. I don't want to be stuck here."

"It is getting cold in here," Frank says. "I'm telling you, this place is haunted."

They both look expectantly at me.

"Tell them or I'll start throwing things. I can do it," the woman warns.

"There's a ghost here," I say.

"In the studio?" Bill asks, looking around. "Where?"

I point to the woman. "She's making the cold breeze you feel. She's waving her arms. She wants me to cross her over."

Bill and Frank are speechless for a moment. The breeze picks up a paper from the table and blows it across the room. They both rock back in their chairs.

"A paper just flew off the table," Bill says into the microphone. "That was creepy."

The woman is still shouting. I try to calm her down. "I can't right now. I'll come back later, and we can do it properly," I tell her, trying to stay away from the mic.

"You're talking to someone right now," Frank says.

Mickey is looking to where I directed my comment, her arms wrapped around herself against the falling temperatures. "We'll come back. We promise. Just stop the cold."

The woman suddenly stops waving and the breeze dies down.

"You'll help me?" she asks.

"We'll help, but not now. Please, stop," I say gently.

The room grows still. Bill and Frank are staring at me in shock.

Bill recovers first. "Did that just happen right here? You were talking to something."

"There's a woman here. She wants our help. She's quite insistent."

"I just want to get out of here. I've been here for so long. You have no idea what it's like," the woman says. "I can't take it anymore."

"What does she look like?" Frank asks.

"She's blonde, really light blonde. Middle-aged. About my height."

"Patty?" Bill asks.

The woman turns her head quickly. "That's my name."

"She says that's her name."

"Patty Strunk?" Bill says.

The woman nods. "That's me."

"That's her. Do you know her?" I ask.

"Patty Strunk used to work here years ago. I heard about her when I first started. She was struck by lightning out in the parking lot and died."

"And I've been stuck in this place ever since," Patty says.

"And now she's haunting the studio," Frank says. "Bloody brilliant!" he adds with a heavy British accent, his trademark phrase.

"Wow, a little taste of *Beyond the Dead* right here in the studio. You're right, Frank, bloody brilliant!"

The show continues for a few more minutes. Patty behaves herself so I can focus on my answers. I manage not to make a fool of myself.

"We understand you often help the police on murder cases too," Bill says. "Can't you just ask the victim's ghost who killed them? Seems pretty easy."

"It doesn't work like that. Often, they have no idea what happened. Or they're not ghosts."

"Are you helping with the murder of that young woman that was found under a bridge?" Frank asks.

"Sort of, maybe," I hedge.

"Rylan found the body," Mickey says. "We were led to it by a ghost that haunts the bridge. Her name is Hazel."

"Hazel haunts the bridge and led you to the body. Can't she just tell you what happened?" Frank asks.

"She didn't see the actual murder. She just found Kenzie."

"The dead finding the dead," Frank says. "Bloody brilliant." This time he says it with wonder.

The British accent makes me think of the British man we saw with Kenzie's friend Meera. For some reason, it makes me think of the tattoos on the girls' hips as well.

I look at Mickey.

"It's a date!"

Mickey is perplexed. "What's a date?" she asks.

"The tattoo. It's a British date. The day, the month, then the year. Seventeenth, June, twenty-one."

"Are you talking about the case?" Bill asks. "Are we seeing you at work?"

"Kind of, maybe. I'm sorry, I just realized something that might be important."

Mickey is already on her phone, googling. "That's what I thought. That's the date Miles Crandall killed himself."

Mickey and I stare at each other as I say, "There has to be a connection."

TWENTY-NINE

RYLAN FLYNN

I own one black dress. The dress I wore to Mom's funeral. As Onyx watches from the bed, I pull it over my head. It falls just below the knee and has long sleeves. It's a little heavy for this time of year, but it'll have to do.

I still have the same shoe problem I had last night. My sneakers will not work, and all my sandals have mysteriously disappeared.

Down the hall, I hear Mom telling Elsa a story. I suddenly remember she has an entire closet full of clothes that she doesn't need.

I knock on the door frame. Mom and Elsa look up from where they're sitting on the bed. "Can I come in?" For some reason, I feel awkward, like I'm intruding on their special time.

"Of course. Why would you even ask?" Mom says.

"Miss Margie is telling me a story about Clifford the Big Red Dog. I thought I knew all the Clifford stories, but this one is new."

"She's pretty good at making up stories," I say. "Hey, Mom, can I borrow some shoes?" I make my way to the closet.

"Where are you going, all dressed up? Do you have another date?" Mom asks, a suggestive tone in her voice.

I stop midway across the room. "Another date?"

"You didn't come home last night. Only makes sense you stayed at Ford's."

"How do you know about that?"

"Honey, I may be dead, but I'm not blind. You've been in love with that man most of your life, and you've been spending lots of time with him. Only makes sense that's where you stayed all night."

"I could have been at Mickey's." I'm not sure I like this newly aware Mom. It's a bit unsettling.

"Is Ford the nice man that was with you when I was still in the bear?" Elsa asks. "I like him."

"Yes, that's Ford. Yes, I was with him last night. Now can you two just go back to your story?" I dig in the closet and find a pair of black flats that will work.

"Did you kiss him?" Elsa pushes.

"That's not any of our business," Mom says knowingly. "Seriously, where are you going all dressed up in the middle of the day?"

"To Kenzie's funeral." The fun energy in the room turns somber.

"Who's Kenzie?" Elsa asks, her voice tiny.

"She's Ford's cousin. She died recently."

"How'd she die?" Elsa asks, innocently curious.

"She was killed."

"Oh no," Elsa says. "That's bad."

"We're trying to catch the one who hurt her. They have her boyfriend in custody, but we don't think he did it."

"Who do you think did?" Mom asks.

"We don't have a name yet, but we'll figure it out."

The corners of Mom's mouth tick up.

"What?" I ask.

"You keep saying 'we'. I like it. It suits you."

"You sound like Mickey." I head for the door. "Thanks for the shoes."

"Not like I'll be wearing them again. Always just this nightgown."

There's no proper response to a ghost's fashion options, so I leave them to their story.

Ford and I drive to the funeral together in his Malibu. As soon as I'm in the car, he asks me about what I said on the show.

"You think the tattoo that Kenzie and Meera have is a date written the British way?" he asks.

"It makes sense. That's the day Miles died. They were friends. Why not mark the date? Lots of people do that."

"But why in the British format? Why not the usual way? It's like they're trying to hide it," he says.

"Their friend Paul is British. Maybe that has something to do with it. Maybe they thought it was cool to be different. They were just kids, who knows why they do what they do."

"If it is a tribute to Miles, why did Meera try to hide it from you?"

"Maybe we could ask her. She'll be at the funeral, I'm sure."

"You act like you're still working the case. Eli is in jail for the murder, remember?" he points out.

"I know. It's just the mystery of the tattoo is really bugging me. It really must have meant something to Kenzie, and to whoever cut it off her. Why would Eli do that?"

"True." He pulls into the parking lot of the funeral home—we're shocked by the number of cars already here. "Wonderful," Ford says in awe. "I'm so glad Kenzie is being remembered like this."

"Do you really think all these people knew her?" I look at the sea of cars, not an open spot left.

"Whether they knew her or knew *of* her, I'm just glad there's a big turnout."

We end up having to park on the street and walk to the funeral home. The receiving line is all the way out the double glass doors. We take our place and settle in for a long wait. People line up behind us as we slowly edge forward.

Ford scans the crowd.

I keep my eyes on the ground.

My back is tingling, and I'm sure there's at least one ghost around.

Ford notices my attention on the ground and takes my hand in his. "You okay?"

"I'm sensing spirits," I say, the tingle growing uncomfortable.

He squeezes my hand. "Do you want to go? I can take you home and come back."

"No. I can't let what I am dictate what I do. I'll be fine."

I lift my eyes and see an old man just inside the glass doors, looking out of place, staring into the parking lot.

"Is there a man looking out the door?" I ask.

Ford checks. "Not that I can see. Is that the spirit you're sensing?"

"I think so." I rub my back.

"It really is a gift and a curse, isn't it? I heard the show this morning. That had to be wild to have a ghost talking to you while you were trying to focus on the interview."

"It can be a challenge, that's for sure."

He grows quiet and we shuffle forward to the door. A few minutes later, he asks, "Would you change it?"

I'd been trying to ignore the ghost a few feet away, so I'm not sure what he means. "Change what?"

"So you couldn't see them. So you weren't plagued everywhere you go."

"I've never thought about it. God gave me this gift. I don't think I can get rid of it, short of moving into the wilderness to be away from them," I try to tease.

"I'm serious. If you could no longer see ghosts, would you choose that?"

I look at the old man, who's turned his head at the word ghost. I don't want him to know.

Then I think of Mom and Elsa at home. No gift means no Mom, and Elsa would still be trapped in the bear.

"I don't think so. It has its perks. Plus, the ghosts need me."

The couple in front of us try to look casual, but I can tell they're listening.

"Maybe we should talk about something else." I turn my eyes back to the floor as we enter the funeral home. "That's better," I say about the air conditioning. "I was getting hot out there in the sun."

Now that we're in the building, Ford scans the line ahead of us. "There's Meera. Looks like she's here with her parents."

"Do you see the British guy? Is he with her?" I try to see ahead, but I'm too short to look above the crowd.

"He's here, but further up the line."

"Hopefully, we can talk to them," I say. "That's not tacky, is it?"

"I've learned that, in a murder investigation, tact takes a backseat to finding the truth."

The door where the ghost is standing opens, and Tyler walks in with a beautiful Black woman right behind. I assume she must be the new partner, Faith Hudson.

He walks directly to Ford.

"I was looking for you," he says, all serious. "I wanted you to hear it from me. They let Eli Graber go."

"What?" Ford asks.

"Why?" I ask.

Tyler turns his attention to me. "Keaton just called. The DA is releasing him on lack of evidence."

"But I thought you had DNA," Ford says.

"We do, but Marrero says there's no sign of sexual assault, so the DNA is irrelevant."

"What about the tipster that saw Eli with her?" Ford asks, shifting on his feet.

"According to Keaton, that's not enough to hold him. He has no priors, no history of violence, nothing besides being Kenzie's boyfriend and the anonymous tip. And he's right. The evidence is weak, and the more I look at it, the less convinced I am that Eli Graber is our man."

"So you think the killer's still out there?" Ford asks.

"Worse," Faith chimes in. "He's probably here at the funeral."

THIRTY

RYLAN FLYNN

"So, what do we do?" I ask.

"We watch," Ford says. "If he's here, he might give himself away by the smallest out-of-the-ordinary action."

I look around. Just in this hall there are tons of people, let alone the ones behind us, and the room-full in front of us. "How do we watch everyone?"

"Normally, we'd have several plain-clothes officers, but we thought this case was tied up, so we don't have anyone here," Tyler says. "It's just us."

"But you took Ford off the case," I point out.

"I didn't have anything to do with that," Tyler says, sounding a little hurt at my accusation.

"We'll worry about that later," Ford steps out of the line. "Let's mingle and keep our eyes peeled. Tyler and Faith, you guys take the hall and the back of the main room. Rylan and I will work the casket area and the front of the room."

Faith looks to Tyler for confirmation.

"Sounds like a plan," Tyler says. "I'll take the back. Faith, you watch the hall."

"I'll sit on that bench and look like I'm just resting. Let's meet back here after the service and compare notes," Faith says.

"It's a plan," Ford says, and we enter the main room.

The room is packed with people, a low buzz of conversation floating in the air. At the very front, surrounded by flower arrangements, is the casket holding Kenzie. Her mother, Julia, stands by the head of the casket. She looks much more worn than when we talked to her before. Paler, her eyes haunted.

My heart goes out to her. It's nice to have all these people to pay their respects, but how exhausting it must be.

Beside her stands Owen and Tammy. They don't seem to be faring any better, as they hug mourner after mourner.

I have to look away. I once stood in their place, Keaton next to me. We had to make small talk to strangers and keep a brave face, when all I wanted to do was fall to the floor and cry.

It was brutal.

After, I went to Mom's house, lay on the bed and let the tears come. I cried until I felt I'd broken something inside.

That's when Mom's ghost first appeared. She sat on the edge of the bed and asked, "Why are you crying? Did someone die?" I thought she meant it as a joke.

It made me cry harder.

The hole in her head was visible from where I was. "Does it hurt?" I asked.

"Does what hurt?" She had no idea.

I didn't tell her.

I shake myself back to the present, standing near the wall where I can watch the room but be out of the way. Ford stands near the other wall—Tyler is in the back.

Soft music plays along with a slideshow of Kenzie. I watch the photos changing but have to tear my eyes away. Seeing the little girl grow into a young woman is heartbreaking. No new pictures of Kenzie will ever be taken. The ones on the screen are all that's left of her life.

That and the memories.

I need to focus. Now that I'm away from the old man near the door, my back isn't hurting. As far as I can tell, there are no other ghosts nearby.

I wish Kenzie's ghost would appear and tell me what happened.

I watch the crowd, not sure what I'm looking for. How does a guilty person act at a funeral? I have no idea. I can only hope I'll recognize it when I see it.

As I watch, Meera and her parents approach the casket. Meera barely even looks at Kenzie, keeping her eyes to the side. I can't blame her. Looking in a casket at a dead body seems like a horrible custom to me. One I avoid as much as possible.

Meera hugs Kenzie's parents and exchanges a few words, then quickly walks away to take a seat in the back to wait for the service.

Nearly all the seats are taken, and workers dressed in suits are putting up more chairs. Soon the room is full to capacity— it's standing-room only.

Making it hard to watch the crowd for suspicious behavior.

And hard for me to see Grandma Delia approach. "I thought that was you, Rylan. Why are you standing over here all alone?" she asks. "Ford is over there."

"I know, we came together. We're kind of working."

"I thought they caught the monster already. What's left to work on?"

"They let him go this afternoon. Not enough evidence to hold him, and the police aren't convinced he did it."

Delia steps next to me, scanning the room. "So you're looking for someone that looks guilty."

"That's the plan. Honestly, I don't know what I'm looking for."

"What about that one?" She points to the British friend of Meera's. "He looks like he's up to something."

"Good eye. I've been wanting to talk to him. I feel like he's involved somehow. Did you know Kenzie and Meera have matching tattoos of a date? It's the date that their friend supposedly committed suicide, at the same bridge Kenzie was found under."

This piques her attention. "You don't say."

"It's in the British format, though. And that guy you just pointed out has a British accent. Plus, Hazel, the ghost at the bridge, has seen him at the bridge with Kenzie."

"Sounds like we should go talk to him," Delia says.

"But the service is about to start."

"They won't start until the line gets shorter. We have plenty of time."

Delia leads the way through the crowd to the man in question. She doesn't hesitate a step, just walks right up to him and says, "So I understand you were friends with my granddaughter."

The man seems a little startled at the sudden intrusion on his conversation with another young man.

"I was friends with Kenzie, if that's what you mean," he says in a smooth accent. "So were a lot of people here. I'm Paul Earnest." He holds out a hand to shake, but Delia ignores it.

"I heard you used to hang out with her at the bridge. That's a bit curious," she says.

"The bridge is a popular hangout," Paul says stiffly. "Look, I'm sorry for your loss. We all are, but I don't understand why you're singling me out."

"Kenzie's tattoo is a British date. You're British. That's a big coincidence," I say.

"I am. But I don't have anything to do with her tattoo."

"Or Meera's?" I push.

"Those girls were always up to something. Why don't you ask Meera what it's about."

The young man Paul was talking to snickers. "I think you're barking up the wrong tree here," he says.

"And who are you?" I counter, not liking being laughed at, or the slight scent of cigarettes coming off the young man.

"I'm Caleb. Another friend of Kenzie's. Like Paul said, a lot of us were."

"From what I hear, she didn't have many friends," I say.

"Look around," Caleb says. "What do you think?"

"I think I have my eye on you—both of you," Delia says.

"For what? They already caught the killer, that Amish guy. Neither of us hurt Kenzie," Paul says.

"They don't have anyone behind bars anymore. They let him go."

They both look shocked.

"We didn't do anything," Caleb says firmly.

"Did you know Miles Crandall?" I ask, changing tactics.

"Of course. Everyone knew Miles. That was horrible what he did to himself," Paul says.

"What's your point?" Caleb asks, growing irritated.

"Why would he choose that bridge to hang himself? I understood that you all liked it there."

"You'd have to ask him," Paul says. "You can talk to ghosts, can't you? I've heard about you. Even heard you on the radio earlier. Stick to hunting ghosts, and not killers."

"In case you hadn't noticed," Caleb says, "this is a funeral. I don't think this is appropriate. We've already talked to the police, now please leave us alone."

"Come on, Rylan. These boys are useless to us," Delia says, leading me away by the arm.

As we take our places back by the wall, Ford approaches. "You two being detectives now?" he asks. "You're supposed to just watch, not confront anyone."

"That Paul Earnest looks guilty to me," Delia says. "I just have a feeling."

"Maybe. But, if you're right, you can't just go at him like that. It could be dangerous."

"I'm not afraid of that little puke," Delia says with surprising venom. "I've seen kids like him. Entitled and spoiled."

"Entitled isn't the same thing as guilty," Ford points out.

The music and slideshow stop, catching our attention.

"Looks like the service is starting," Delia says. "Rylan, you and Ford sit up here with us."

"Looks like you've won Grandma over," Ford says near my ear. "I knew she'd like you."

THIRTY-ONE
RYLAN FLYNN

I appreciate Grandma Delia's invitation to sit in the front row, but I'm not comfortable about it. This row is for family—close family. I feel like an impostor sitting here. I've never even met Kenzie.

Finding her lifeless body doesn't count.

Still, this is where Ford belongs, and I'm happy to support him however he needs. The service is lovely, but it's also heart-wrenching. The pastor gives a speech, mentioning the high-lights of Kenzie's life. It's pitifully short. The girl barely had a chance to live. He finishes with a prayer and, as we bow our heads, Ford grasps my hand in his.

When we raise our heads, Meera walks up to the podium near the casket. She takes a long moment to look at Kenzie, tears streaming. She takes so long that the crowd begins to shift uncomfortably.

She turns a wet face to the crowd and says, "Kenzie was my friend. The best friend I could ever have had." She wipes her eyes and continues singing Kenzie's praises, sharing little stories of their times together. It is a moving tribute that brings many to tears.

"I love you, Kenzie," Meera finishes, then takes her seat and lifts her chin. She sits there stoically staring at a wall, obviously fighting emotions.

The service concludes. We all stand and begin to shuffle toward the doors.

"Let's hang back and watch the crowd some more. He has to be here," Ford says. I follow him back to the wall where I stood earlier. It's hard to see anything in the sea of moving bodies. A few mourners approach the casket, saying their final farewells. I watch each one carefully, searching for any scrap of guilt they might show.

Nothing seems out of place—everyone is somber and respectful. To be fair, I don't know how a killer might act in this situation.

We watch as the room clears, and soon the only people left are the immediate family near the front. We join them and Ford hugs everyone. I smile shyly and hang back, feeling like I'm imposing on a private moment.

Tyler and Faith are the only ones left in the room besides family. Kenzie's dad, Owen, notices them waiting.

"Why are the police here?" Owen asks Ford. "I thought they already caught my daughter's killer. He's in jail. They told me."

"Eli Graber was released today. They're pretty sure he didn't do it."

"Oh, he didn't do it," Julia says. "Kenzie loved the boy. I can't imagine he'd hurt her."

"They think the killer was here at the funeral?" Owen asks.

"It happens. We're just looking for anything unusual. Anyone acting strangely."

"Everyone acts strangely at a funeral." Tammy joins the conversation. "It's so awful, you don't know what to do with yourself." She clasps and unclasps her hands.

"Did anyone stand out to you?" Ford asks the group. "Anything at all?"

"I saw some of Kenzie's friends talking down the hall when I went to get a water," Julia says. "They were all huddled together and whispering. They stopped when they saw me."

"Who was it?" Ford asks.

"I don't know their names, except Meera. They're friends from Ashby. Two boys."

"Gray shirt, gray tie?" I ask, thinking of Paul.

"I think so. The other had on khakis and a black shirt," Julia says.

"That's the two young men we were talking to, Paul and Caleb," Delia pipes in.

"Why would they be whispering?" Owen asks.

"Could mean nothing," Ford hedges. "They're friends, maybe they just wanted a moment together, out of sight of the crowd."

"Or they're planning something," Delia says.

"What could they be planning?" Julia asks.

"Whatever young people plan," Delia says vaguely. "I just know they are up to no good."

"You think they hurt Kenzie?" Owen asks.

"Maybe. I mean, I don't want to think that, but someone did. Someone who knew her," Delia says, looking to Ford for help.

"We can't jump to conclusions," Ford says. "We need to stick to the evidence. So far, we don't have much. Kids talking in a hall is not evidence."

"But you will check out this Paul and Caleb?" Delia asks.

Tyler has been quietly listening to the conversation from a few feet away but joins the group to answer. "We've already checked them out. They were together the night Kenzie was taken. They were at Paul's place playing video games."

"So they have alibis," Delia says, disappointed. "Who does that leave?"

"We're still working on the case," Faith joins in. "We have a few leads to follow still."

"Then get on it," Owen says. "Find out who took my baby girl."

After saying his final goodbye to his cousin at her casket, Ford walks out of the funeral home with a determined look on his face. Tyler and Faith join us just outside the front doors. The old-man ghost is still looking out of those doors. I wonder if he can leave the building, or if he's tied to it. I think about talking to him, but this doesn't seem like the right time. I add him to the mental list of ghosts I need to come back to, souls I need to help. I feel like the list just keeps getting longer.

I'll think about that later. Right now, Ford needs my full attention.

I turn my back on the old man.

"So, what do you want to do now?" Ford asks Tyler. "What leads do you still have to track down?"

"We don't really have any," Tyler says, looking at the ground.

"I just said that to make the family feel better," Faith says. "We've talked to everyone we know about. School friends, all the family, people she worked with, all her neighbors. No one saw anything helpful."

"I'm sorry," Tyler says to Ford. "I don't know where else to look. Eli looked good for it. His DNA and everything."

"What about the tip? Can't you trace that?"

"We tried, but no luck."

Ford shifts, frustrated. "There has to be something we can do. What about the Amish? Maybe one of Eli's family did it.

They could have been upset he was dating an English woman and decided to get rid of her."

"We looked into that too," Tyler says. "All his family have been accounted for. No one was anywhere near Ashby that night."

Ford runs his hand through his hair. "There has to be something we can do," he repeats.

"Hopefully, there will be a break," Tyler says. "I'm not giving up, but, as for today, I don't know what else there is."

Silence falls over our little group.

"So that's it?" I ask.

"For now," Tyler says.

We stand in awkward silence for another few moments.

"I guess I'll take you home," Ford says to me.

"Okay," I say, guarded. I don't really want to go home alone. I'd hoped to spend the day with him.

Especially after last night.

"Thanks for all you've done," he says to Tyler and Faith. "I know you're working hard. Just don't give up on her."

"We aren't," Faith says.

Ford places a hand on my back and gently leads me to the car.

"I'm sorry, but I think I just need to be alone," he says as we drive toward my house. "All this is a lot."

"I get it." And I do. "Funerals are exhausting under the best of circumstances."

He stares straight ahead, driving silently until we're outside my house.

"Thanks for coming. Really. I'm glad you were there."

"I'm glad I could be there with you." I squeeze his hand—a kiss just doesn't seem right.

"I'll call you later," he says, sounding so sad it hurts my heart.

"Take care and get some rest." I don't know what else to say.

I get out of the car and watch him drive away, then let myself in the back door.

Mom and Elsa are together in her room. Onyx sits on the bed, with them but not with them. I wonder if he even knows they're in the room.

"Hi, Rylan," Elsa says when she sees me at the door. "Did you know, if we try really hard, we can make things move?"

"I know. Pretty cool," I say.

"We've been practicing." Elsa uses the tip of her finger to push a lipstick tube across Mom's dressing table.

"That's great," I tell her.

"How'd it go?" Mom asks, concerned.

"Not great. They let Eli go, and now they don't know who hurt Kenzie."

"I'm so sorry. What are you going to do now?"

I take a deep breath. "Nothing. We don't know where to go from here. Hopefully, tomorrow we'll find a direction to go."

"This isn't your case, honey. Not your responsibility."

"But I feel like it is. God led me to find her. Now I need Him to lead me to her killer."

"Why don't you go change and join us? We can watch some TV and take your mind off things."

That sounds heavenly.

"Hey, Rylan?" Elsa calls as I turn to walk down the hall.

"Yeah?"

"What makes that horrible noise in the next room? It's scary."

"I told her I don't hear anything," Mom says. "Must be her imagination."

"I didn't imagine it. It's a horrible sound."

I don't want to go into it now, so I say, "I'll look into it."

"I wanted to go in there, but Miss Margie said I shouldn't."

"Elsa, you stay out of that room," I snap. "It's dangerous."

Elsa stares at me, startled. "I won't," she says.

But I don't believe her. Tell a kid not to do something and it's the first thing they do once your back is turned.

THIRTY-TWO

I look at the date tattooed on my hip.

It was a bad idea. All of ours were.

I thought the reminder would keep us quiet.

It only drove Kenzie to tell.

I had to silence her. There was no other way.

The memory of feeling her thin neck beneath my hands makes my heart race. I had time to enjoy the moment, to savor it.

Not like with Miles. That time it happened too fast. I hadn't meant to hurt him.

But he touched Kenzie.

He deserved it.

She was mine.

Now my face was the last one she saw. No one can take that from me.

I look at the tattoo, my memorial to Miles's death, and it seems to itch.

Kenzie's tattoo sits in front of me, suspended in a jar of alcohol. They cremated Kenzie today. All that's left of her on earth is this scrap of skin that matches mine.

I touch the jar and grin.

194 DAWN MERRIMAN

I'll have her forever.

The keychain—a large crescent moon—begins to glow like it glowed the night I took Kenzie.

"Get rid of her. She's too close," it says.

It doesn't take me long to realize who "she" is.

She's bound to figure it out. She knows what the tattoo means. Figured out it's a date.

My hands flex, thinking of Miles's neck beneath my squeezing fingers.

Then of Kenzie's.

Rylan Flynn's face takes the place of theirs.

"I'll take care of her," I tell the keychain. The plan is already in motion—I'm ready again.

THIRTY-THREE

RYLAN FLYNN

I lie on Mom's bed, watching reruns of *The Big Bang Theory*. Onyx is at the foot of the bed, and Elsa and Mom are next to me sitting against the headboard. I've seen all the episodes several times and find the familiarity soothing. Soon, my eyes grow heavy—I catch my chin drooping.

"You should go to bed," Mom says.

I look out the window. The sun is just starting to go down. "It's still early."

"Not that early. Besides, who would care?"

I only debate a moment. It's been a long day.

My phone sits on the bedspread next to me, and it rings as I reach for it.

Unknown Caller on the screen.

"Probably a sales call," I say and send the call to voicemail.

Before I even get out of the room, the phone rings again. With a heavy sigh, I answer. "Hello?"

"Is this Rylan Flynn?" a female voice asks.

"Yes," I answer, annoyed.

"This is Meera. You know, Kenzie's friend." She sounds upset.

My annoyance disappears, replaced with trepidation. "Meera, why are you calling? How did you get this number?"

"I need you to meet me. It's important."

"At your apartment?"

"No. Right now, at the bridge. You know, the one where Kenzie was found."

"Meera, are you in trouble? You should call the police."

"I don't need the police. Just come and I'll explain it, all of it. I know what happened to Kenzie."

"Then you need to call the police right now. Meera? Meera?"

She's hung up.

I look at Mom and Elsa in shock. "I need to go."

"What was that about?" Mom asks. "It sounded bad."

"Kenzie's best friend says she needs me to meet her at the bridge. Said it's important and I need to come now. She sounded scared."

"You should wait and take Ford."

"I'll call him, but he wanted to be alone for a while. Look, I'll be fine. It's just Meera."

"Rylan, this is ill-advised. You should take someone with you."

"There's no time." I hurry from the room.

"Let us come with you," Mom says. "We can help."

"Yeah, let us come," Elsa says.

"I guess nothing can hurt you now. Fine. Come along." I make my way through the paths to the front door.

"I know this is not the time," Mom says, "but I've been meaning to tell you, you need to clean this mess. It's not good."

"I know, I know. I will. Just come on."

"At least call Ford," Mom says as we climb into the car. "Let him know what's going on."

I place the call, but after several rings it goes to voicemail.

"I'm meeting Meera at the bridge. She says she needs to tell me all of it. Come when you can." I hang up.

"There, happy?"

"No. I still think you should wait and take him with you."

"Just come on."

Mom and Elsa crush into the front seat together. I drive toward Ostermeyer Road and the bridge. The sun has set and it's fully dark when we get there.

Ahead, there is a compact car parked near the bridge, the inside cab light on. Meera turns around and looks right into our headlights from the front seat.

"There she is," I say, parking behind her.

Now that we're here, my nerves are in full force. Mom's right, maybe this is a bad idea.

I check my phone, but there's nothing from Ford.

I send him a quick text.

Can you meet me at the bridge? Meera wants to talk.

I put the phone away. Meera gets out of her car and approaches my window.

"I'm so glad you came," she says, a little out of breath. "Let's go on the bridge and I'll tell you everything."

The frogs are singing loudly—the moon is full and bright in a cloudless sky. Mom and Elsa follow as we walk to the bridge. It's almost peaceful, if only my belly wasn't swimming and my heart pounding.

We reach the bridge, and I say, "What did you want to tell me?" I look around for Hazel, but I don't see her.

"I want to tell you what happened here," Meera starts in a soft voice.

"Why me?"

"Because you're going to figure it out. I heard you on the

radio this morning, when you figured out the tattoo is the date that Miles died. It's only a matter of time until you learn the rest."

"Why don't you tell me what this is all about." I feel brave with Mom and Elsa behind me.

Meera's face crumples and she begins to cry. "I'm not supposed to tell. It's not part of the plan."

My nerves start to clamor. Is this a setup after all? "Tell me what's going on, Meera."

Meera sniffles and wipes at her nose, then lifts her chin and looks me in the eye. "Miles didn't hang himself. He was killed. They hung him to make it look like suicide."

"Who? Paul and Caleb? Tell me what happened."

"We were here at the bridge like always. Miles put his hand on Kenzie's knee, and Caleb freaked out. He punched Miles, hard. Miles fell down and they jumped him. Paul held him down while Caleb—he—"

"He strangled him?"

"Y-yes," Meera hiccups. "Then they got a rope and made it look like Miles hung himself. Kenzie and I were so scared. Caleb was a wild man, and Paul just helped him." She looks over the side of the bridge where his body would have been. "Caleb made us promise never to tell anyone, and we got the tattoos as a sort of pact. It was Paul's idea to do a British date. He thought it was funny."

"But Kenzie was going to tell," I say, putting the pieces together.

"She was. Then Caleb and Paul—"

"They killed her to keep her quiet."

Meera nods, her hair swinging. "Caleb was so mad, and Paul does anything he says. They went to her apartment and took her and lied that they were together that night."

"You're okay now," I say, trying to calm her.

She looks up suddenly. "None of this was supposed to happen. I'm so sorry. They made me."

"Rylan, behind you!" Elsa cries.

I turn just in time to see two men rushing at me. It's Caleb and Paul.

"Run!" Mom shouts.

I pound down the bridge, Caleb closing in behind.

"Don't hurt her!" Meera cries. "I changed my mind."

"Shut up!" Paul yells. "Or I'll kill you too."

"Stop!" Meera screams as Paul descends on her. He grabs her by the hair and drags her to the side of the bridge.

"Please, please don't do this." Meera is sobbing. "None of this is right."

Paul catches her around the waist. "We should have silenced you too," he says as he picks her up. Meera kicks and breaks free, but Paul catches her a few steps later. He lifts her over the side of the bridge and, kicking and shouting, Meera falls into the water.

"Look, I won't tell anyone about this," I try as Caleb catches up to me. "Just let me go and we can forget all about it."

Caleb laughs, high and wild. "Nice try, ghost hunter. You should have minded your own business. You should have left that little tramp where we put her."

I back to the side of the bridge, facing them both down. "Why did you kill her? What did she ever do to you?"

"She was going to talk. That boyfriend of hers was making her change into something soft. We made a pact, and she was going to break it," Caleb says.

"You both killed Miles. It wasn't a suicide."

"Meera has a big mouth," Caleb says. "Too bad."

Caleb stalks me, taking a rope from his back pocket. Paul is close behind.

"You don't want to do this," I say, wondering if I should run again. Caleb is tall, his legs long. He'll catch me in a few strides.

"You're right. I'd rather kill you with my bare hands. It worked with Miles. That idiot coroner never knew the difference. But I don't think it will work with you. Better to have only rope marks on that pretty neck."

I glance over the side to the water. Kids come here to jump. Meera fell and survived.

I back away, but Caleb closes in, pressing me against the side of the metal bridge, with Paul by his shoulder.

The wild look in both their eyes convinces me.

Seeing my intent, Mom yells, "Jump!"

I scramble over the side, push off the rail and jump feet first.

I sink through the air, through the darkness.

The late spring water closes over my head and chills me instantly. The shock knocks me hard. I swim toward the surface and finally reach air. The river has drawn me under the bridge and a short way downstream. Further down the bank, I see Meera climbing out of the water.

I'm relieved she's okay, but I stroke hard in the opposite direction, not trusting her.

Something splashes behind me, and I hear Caleb hit the water. Paul is running down the bridge toward the bank.

The cold is pulling at my body—I need to get out of the water before Caleb catches me.

I turn and swim toward the bank.

As I reach the shallow water, where I can touch the bottom, Caleb grabs my ankle.

"Come here. Don't make this harder than it has to be."

Meera is on the other bank, screaming for him to stop.

I kick and pull, but he doesn't let go. I lose my balance and fall into the water.

He jumps on my back, pressing my face into the gravel floor of the river. He holds me there for several moments, then pulls me back into the air by my hair.

"Can't let water in your lungs. It has to look like you hung yourself," he growls. I smack at him, but he grabs one of my wrists in his large hand, twisting it behind my back. I sink below the water, and he pulls me up again.

"Stop fighting," he hisses. "You can't stop me." With his free hand, he wraps the rope around my neck. I shove the fingers of the hand he isn't holding into the loop, desperate to keep the rope from my skin.

"Don't," I beg. "Get off me."

I sink below the surface again—the rope tightens across my neck. He pulls me up, the rope biting my skin.

"Stop him!" Mom cries, trying to wrestle Caleb, but passing right through him.

I hear Meera screaming "stop," but my blood pounds in my ears so loud it seems far away.

I'm alone in the dark water with a maniac.

The rope tightens, bites harder.

Above me, Caleb's face is eerily calm, a serene smile on his lips. The smile makes me buck and kick, but the rope just grows tighter, my lungs burning.

I look away from Caleb to the trees above. If this is the end, I don't want his horrible smiling face to be the last thing I see.

The branches sway as I claw at the rope.

Black dots swim in my vision, then block out the branches.

I close my eyes.

And the rope loosens.

Caleb falls on top of me, the weight of his body shoving me underwater.

I instinctively push him off, raising my head, gasping.

Mom stands over Caleb's body, a rock in her hand. Caleb moans but doesn't move.

"I did it!" she shouts, then drops the rock. "I moved the rock."

Shocked at what she was able to do, I can only stare for a moment.

Caleb is face down in the water.

"Don't kill him!" Meera shouts from the far bank.

I grab Caleb by the back of his shirt and pull him from the water to the bank. I drop him on the muddy ground. I pull the rope from around my sore neck and tie him up.

I'm not gentle, and he moans at the rough handling.

"Shut up," I mumble.

Meera suddenly screams as Paul grabs her by the arm, dragging her toward the water on the far side of the river.

"Let her go!" I shout.

He shoves her face down as she kicks and flails. I dive into the river, intent on swimming across. When I surface, the current has carried me downstream and she's getting further away.

"Help her, Mom!" I scream.

Mom is there in an instant, another rock in her hand.

Paul looks up as the rock flies through the air and smashes into his temple. He collapses on top of Meera, who isn't moving.

I finally reach the other bank. As soon as my feet hit solid ground, I run to her. I push Paul off and he rolls onto the muddy riverside. I flip Meera over, praying she'll be okay.

She isn't moving, her eyes are closed. I pull her onto solid ground and start CPR. I compress her chest, then breathe into her mouth.

"Save her, Rylan. Save her," Mom shouts beside me.

I compress again.

Meera suddenly chokes, and I turn her on her side. Water pours from her mouth and then she gasps to life.

"You did it!" Mom shouts.

"Yay!" Elsa chimes in.

Then I hear splashing nearby. The beam of a flashlight slices through the darkness as Ford calls my name.

The light hurts my eyes, but I'm so happy to see it. Soon,

he's wrapping me in his arms. "Are you okay?" He touches my face, runs his hands over me, looking for injuries.

"I'm okay, thanks to—" I stop short. I can't tell him Mom is here.

Ford searches my face, waiting for me to finish. When I don't, he says, "It doesn't matter, as long as you're safe."

"Caleb and Paul killed Kenzie," I say, rubbing my neck. "They also killed Miles Crandall. They thought Kenzie was going to confess."

Ford looks at the unconscious man in the mud, then at the tied-up man on the other bank. "You did all this?"

"She saved me," Meera says, sitting up in the mud.

Ford looks perplexed, but just shakes his head. "I told you not to do something rash like this. I begged you to stay out of trouble."

"I had to come. Meera needed me."

He seems to want to argue, but just pulls me close instead. "They did it together?" he asks Meera.

She begins to cry. "I'll tell you all about it. Let's just get out of here."

"Wait. I need to see something." I let go of Ford and look in Paul's pockets. He moans as I move him but doesn't wake up. Something hot brushes against my fingertips.

I pull out some keys—a small, round keychain glows green. I put the keychain against a rock, pick up another and smash the light into oblivion.

"What was that for?" Ford asks.

"Didn't you see it glowing?"

"All I saw was a keychain."

"I can't explain now, but I'll tell you everything. Soon."

"Rylan, it's not fair to keep secrets like this."

I meet his eyes, searching them. I see what I need to see and say, "Come over tonight and I'll show you."

Ford searches my face too, then nods slightly.

Paul moans awake. "I didn't do anything," he says.

"You have the right to remain silent. I suggest you use it," Ford barks.

He falls quiet, the only sound we can hear is the frogs and the river.

Soon, sirens join the chorus.

THIRTY-FOUR

RYLAN FLYNN

Once the scene on the bridge is cleared, Caleb and Paul are taken into custody, the rope replaced by metal handcuffs. Meera sobs that she was forced to help them. She's taken in for questioning and possible charges—if I want to press them.

I found a matching keychain in Caleb's pocket and smashed that one too. Ford didn't ask what I was doing. Just turned away.

Tyler and Faith stay behind with Ford and me, the last to leave.

"Looks like you had another close call," Tyler says to me.

"Starting to become a habit, I guess," I say, trying for humor, but rubbing at my sore neck.

"You shouldn't have come alone," Ford says, harsher than I expect after the tender moment we shared earlier. Once the police arrived, he was all business and barely spoke to me. I figured it was just because he was working, but now he seems genuinely angry.

"I called and you didn't answer," I point out.

"I was in the shower. But that's not the point. You can't keep chasing after murderers and nearly getting yourself killed."

"I came to meet Meera. I didn't know it was a trap, that

Caleb and Paul would be here." I raise my chin, growing angry myself.

Mom says, "Now don't lose your cool. He's just worried."

I ignore her.

"I can't protect you if you keep running off like this," he pushes. "You promised to stay safe, to be rational about these situations."

Hearing his tone, Tyler and Faith move away.

"I don't need you to protect me." My voice raises, my adrenaline still pumping. "And I'm not being irrational."

"You were nearly killed. Again."

"You go into danger yourself. What was I supposed to do, sit at home where it's safe?"

"Yes. Stay safe," he says. "Like you promised."

"That's not what I do. I go where I'm needed."

"Then go where the ghosts need you, and don't throw yourself into police business."

I do not like his tone, or his words.

"You can't tell me what to do. You always try, and it never goes well," I warn, bristling.

"I can't stand by and watch you get hurt either." He looks to the moon as if for guidance. After a long, heavy moment, he says, "I don't think I can do this, Rylan."

I grow cold. Colder than I was in the river.

"What are you saying?" My voice is tiny.

"I don't know what I'm saying." He takes several steps toward his car. "I think I just need some time."

Before I can stop him, he turns and walks away. Soon the tail lights of his car are fading away.

Tyler and Faith have the good grace to leave, too, with a few mumbles of apology.

I'm alone on the bridge, except for the dead who surround me.

I stand in the dark for a long time, not wanting to go home—
wanting those last minutes back.

I shouldn't have argued with him.

He's right. Sometimes, I get careless, don't think rationally.

It can't be over. It just started.

"That was hard to watch," Hazel says, suddenly by my side.

"You finally show up," I say, harsher than I intended. "You
missed all the excitement."

"Your mom told me what happened. How crazy."

I turn on her in my hurt and anger. "Where were you? Why
aren't you here watching over things? You could have saved all
this trouble if you'd been here when Kenzie was hurt, or even
when Miles was killed."

Hazel jumps at my harsh tone.

"Don't yell at me. If you must know, I was at the storage units."

Something clicks into place. "With Jeremiah? Jeremiah
Otto? I knew he was hiding something, and so were you. How
long have you been seeing each other?"

"Oh, I don't know. Many winters. I haven't counted. He's
the only thing that makes this existence bearable."

I think of Ford, and know exactly what she means.

"Maybe you should cross over," I suggest.

"That's easy for you to say. Don't you think I want that?
We're just stuck here for eternity."

"I can help you."

"How?"

"It's kind of what I do for the show. Do you want to cross? I
can at least try."

Anything to take my mind from the heartbreak of Ford's
leaving me here.

"I'll be right back," Hazel says, full of excitement.

She disappears, leaving me with Mom and Elsa, who have
witnessed the whole conversation.

"You really think you can cross them?" Mom asks.

I shrug. "It's worth a try."

Soon, Hazel returns with Jeremiah, the ghost from the storage units.

"We came back to try to cross you the other night," I tell him. "You refused."

"I didn't want to leave Hazel," Jeremiah says.

"But you want to cross? To leave this plane?" I push to be sure he understands.

"As long as we're together," he says.

"Stand right there. First, I have to say prayers." I start, reciting from memory what Dad normally says. Mom and Elsa watch with interest.

Nothing happens for a while.

"I don't think this will work," Hazel says.

I feel desperate and keep praying. Soon, my voice breaks.

"Please, God, please take these two souls. Let them be together in the afterlife, as they could never be together in their own lives."

A tiny square of light opens on the bridge.

"It's working!" Mom shouts. "I knew you could do it."

I pray with renewed vigor, the words flowing off my tongue easily. The light grows.

I'm so focused on the ritual, I don't realize that Mom is staring raptly at the light. Until she takes two steps toward it.

She's drawn to it, summoned by it.

"No, Mom. That's not for you!" I scream, terrified she'll step through. She turns to look at me, then back to the light.

For a horrid moment, I think she's going to go.

"Don't leave, Miss Margie," Elsa says, her voice wavering.

She steps back, away.

Hazel grabs Jeremiah by the hand and says, "Let's go." She leads him through the light.

As soon as they are through, the light closes. We stand in the dark.

The three of us don't say anything, just stare at where the light had been.

"That was the most beautiful thing I've ever seen," Mom finally whispers.

"Can we just go home now?" I ask, exhausted, walking to the car.

Elsa walks beside me. "Will I get to go through the light someday? And Miss Margie?"

I don't even want to think of a life without them.

Or a life without Ford.

We drive quietly home. Each of us lost in our thoughts. I wonder if Mom is disappointed that she didn't cross.

I don't want to know the answer, so I don't ask.

I'm lost in my own disappointment and shock. How could I fight with Ford like that? It's so stupid. I try to call him, but it goes to voicemail.

I mumble, "I'm sorry," then hang up.

"These things always work themselves out," Mom says. "Just keep your head up."

I don't answer. My heart is breaking.

Back home, I let myself in the back door. As soon as I step inside, I realize something is different. The energy of the house has changed.

Onyx darts from the hall and pushes against my legs. His tail is bushy and he seems terrified.

"I'm sorry," Elsa says.

I look at the girl in surprise. "For what?"

"I got bored at the bridge with all the police and things. I came here."

Fear grips me—I hurry toward the hall.

"I can move boxes," she says with a mixture of pride and regret.

The boxes in front of Keaton's door are tossed aside. The door hangs open.

THIRTY-FIVE

The match lights easily. Just a quick scratch and the flame flickers to life in my thick fingers.

"Good. That's good," the voice says.

I touch the match to a curtain and the flame crawls onto the fabric. Fingers of orange reach further as the flame spreads. So does the adrenaline in my blood, the excitement building as the fire climbs.

"You did it," the voice says with pride. I know it's behind me, but I'm too afraid to look.

I watch the fire as long as the heat will allow—but still longer than I should. My skin aches and begins to blister.

"Keep watching," the voice commands. I obey, as I always do, growing curious now that the source is with me. The thing behind me laughs as flames lick the body I placed on the floor, the man's hair singeing with a hiss.

"Such a lovely sight," it says.

I have to turn, I have to see the inspiration for my deeds.

"I did this for you," I say and glance over my shoulder.

Its mouth is open and a howl fills the air.

I can't look. I turn away, the smoke choking me.

"Now for another," it says, slipping out of the house, into the night.

I can't breathe, and my skin stings. I follow the thing outside.

I always follow.

A LETTER FROM DAWN

Dearest reader,

A huge thank you for choosing to read *The River Ghost*. I truly appreciate you. I hope you loved it. If you did enjoy it, and want to keep up to date with all my latest releases, just sign up at the following link. Your email address will never be shared and you can unsubscribe at any time.

www.secondskybooks.com/dawn-merriman

Writing *The River Ghost* was a fun ride. Rylan always keeps me on my toes. I'm so glad that she and Ford finally found each other. Too bad it was short-lived. I enjoy bringing Northeast Indiana to all you readers. I hope this book, with the Amish angle, really brought my home area to light.

If you enjoyed *The River Ghost*, I would be very grateful if you could leave a review. Feedback from readers is so special. I'm genuinely interested in what you think, and it makes such a difference helping new readers to discover one of my books for the first time.

Again, thank you for reading *The River Ghost*.

Happy reading and God bless,

Dawn Merriman

KEEP IN TOUCH WITH DAWN

I love hearing from my readers and I interact on my Fan Club on Facebook at the link below. Join the club today and get behind the scenes info on my works, fun games and interesting tidbits from my life.

www.facebook.com/groups/dawnmerrimannovelistfanclub

 facebook.com/dawnmerrimannovelist
 instagram.com/dawnmerrimannovelist

ACKNOWLEDGMENTS

These stories may come from me, but they come to life through the help of "my team."

First, I'd like to thank my husband, Kevin. He has great ideas that truly inspire my stories. His unwavering support gets me through the sticky plot points. His patience while I talk about Rylan and the gang and what they are up to is amazing.

To my beta reader team—Carlie Frech, Katie Hoffman, Jamie Miller, and Candy Wajer—your insights on *The River Ghost* were invaluable. Thank you for taking the time to read the rough pages.

A huge thank you to Bookouture and Second Sky Books and the wonderful team there. My editor, Jack Renninson, has been a huge help as always. Jack, thank you for all the suggestions that made *The River Ghost* what it is today.

Thank you to my readers for choosing my stories to spend time with.

Most of all, thank you to God for giving me the gift to tell these stories. I hope I do them justice.

Thank you all,

Dawn Merriman

PUBLISHING TEAM

Turning a manuscript into a book requires the efforts of many people. The publishing team at Bookouture would like to acknowledge everyone who contributed to this publication.

Audio
Alba Proko
Sinead O'Connor
Melissa Tran

Commercial
Lauren Morrissette
Hannah Richmond
Imogen Allport

Cover design
Damonza.com

Data and analysis
Mark Alder
Mohamed Bussuri

Editorial
Jack Renninson
Melissa Tran

Printed in Great Britain
by Amazon